The Usborne

Big Drawing Book

Pictures drawn by
Josephine Thompson
and Caroline Day

Words written
by Fiona Watt

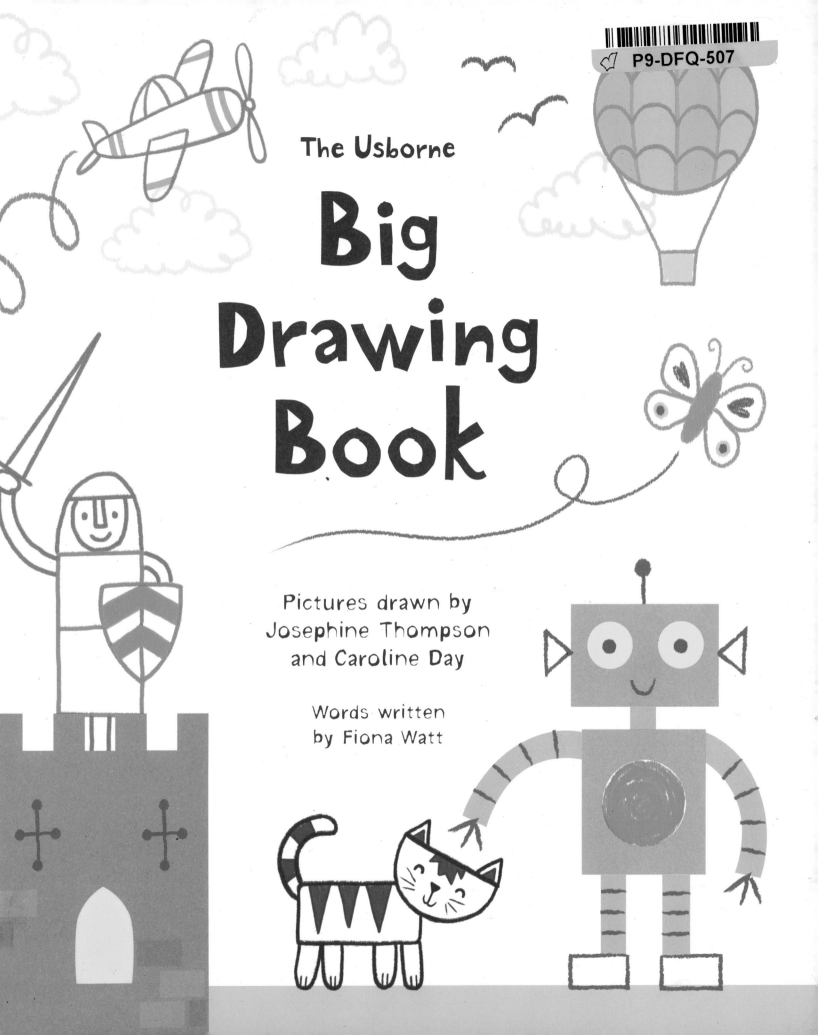

Draw snails and bugs hiding on leaves.
1
A long body...
2
a spiral shell...
3
feelers and a mouth.

Every big leaf needs a snail or a bug!
1
An oval body...
2
eyes and lines...
3
legs, spots and a smile.

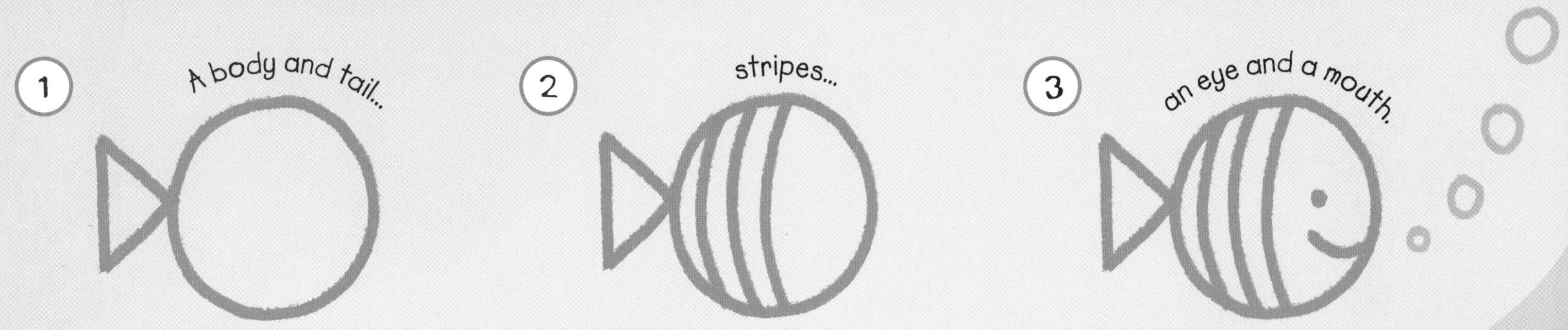
1
A body and tail...
2
stripes...
3
an eye and a mouth.

Draw fish swimming in a coral reef.

Glug...glug...

Draw buzzing bees and fluttering butterflies.

1
A body...
2
wings...
3
an eye and stripes.

Buzzzzzz

1
A body...
2
four wings...
3
and feelers.

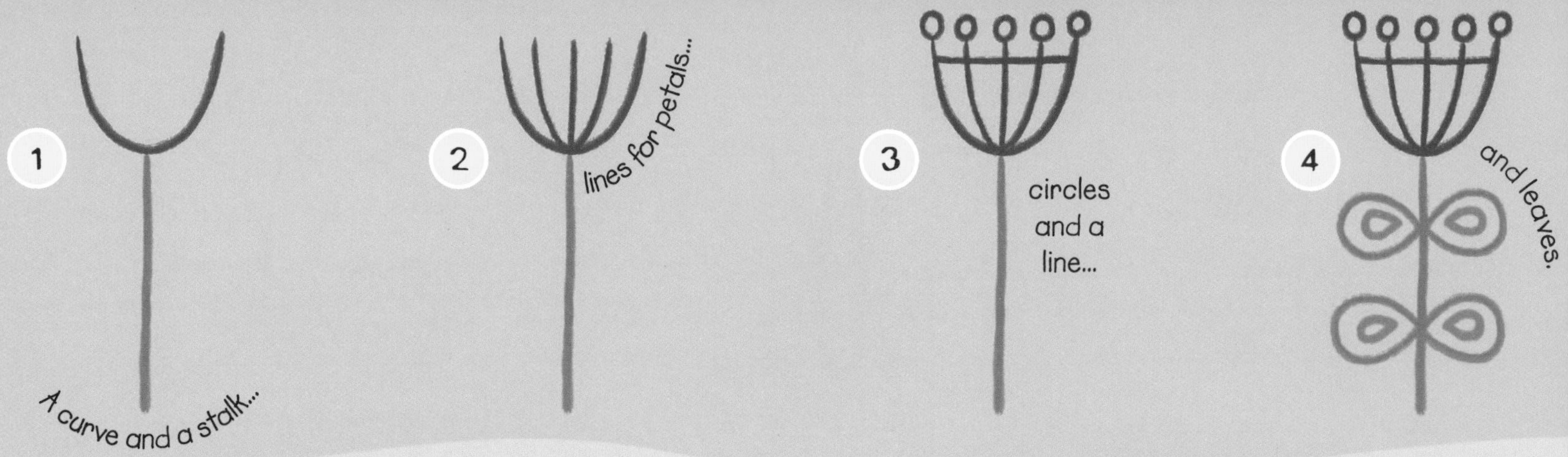
1
A curve and a stalk...
2
lines for petals...
3
circles and a line...
4
and leaves.

Draw plants in the pots.

1
A circle...
2
lots of petals...
3
dots and
a stalk...
4
two leaves.

1
Two lines like this...
2
a curved tummy...
3
a head...

Squawk!

Draw birds on the branches.

4
a beak and an eye...
5
a wing and claws...
6
and a long tail.

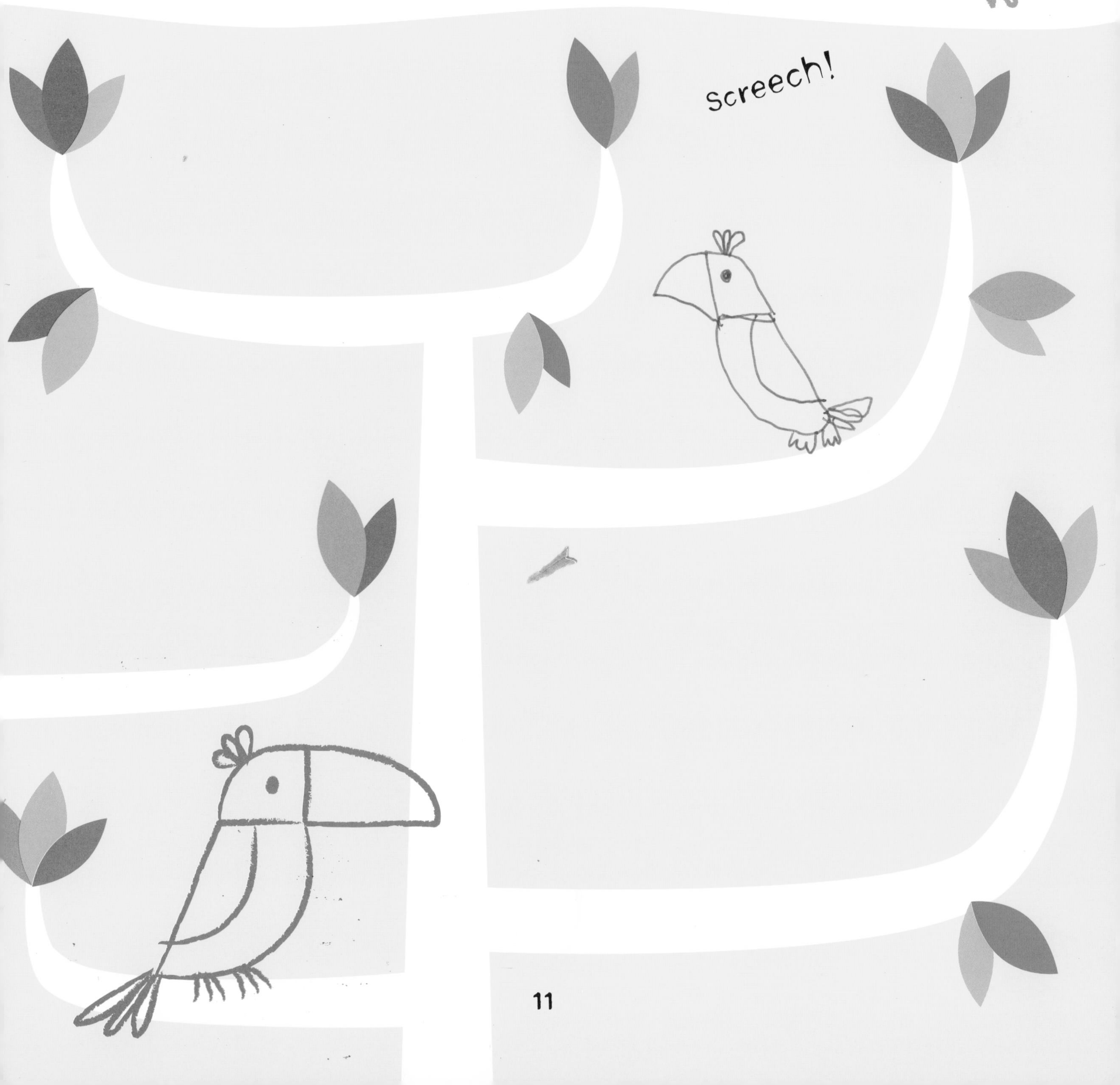

Screech!

1
A rectangle and a triangle...
2
two small rectangles...
3
four little triangles...
4
and flames.

Draw rockets and planets in space.

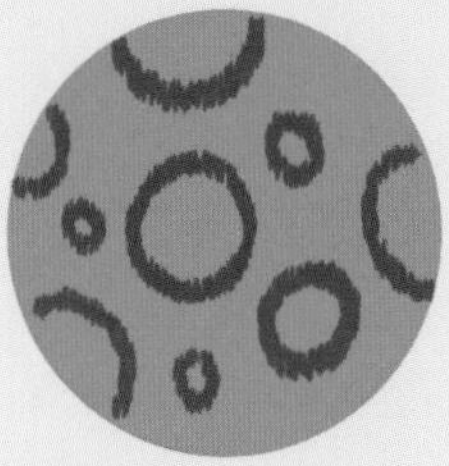

Ideas for different planets

Whoooooooooosh!

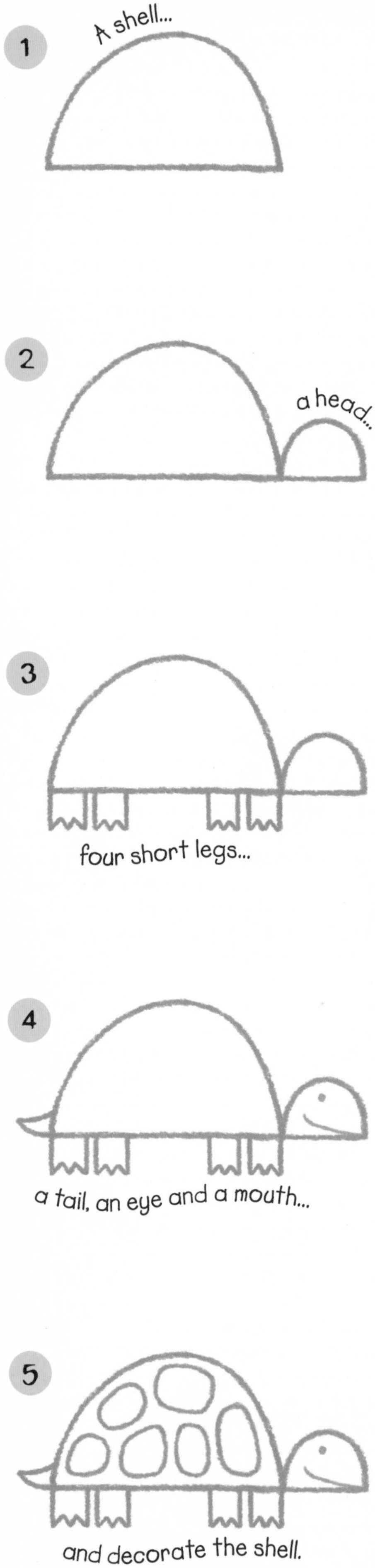

1
A shell...
2
a head...
3
four short legs...
4
a tail, an eye and a mouth...
5
and decorate the shell.

Draw tortoises with patterned shells.

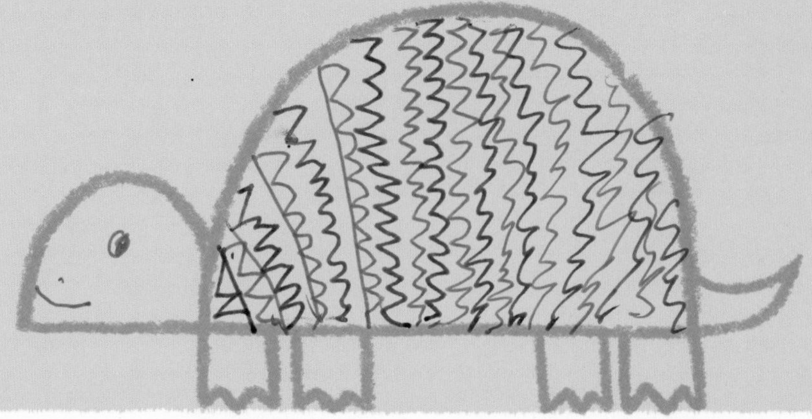

Please give me a head and a tail.
Hello!

1
A head and body...
2
arms and legs...
3
two ears...
a tummy and tail...
4
a face and some hair.

Draw monkeys swinging from the vines.

Ee...ee...ee...
MOMMY
Mayla
Marack
daddY
Draw some baby monkeys, too

Try horns and big teeth...

lots of eyes...

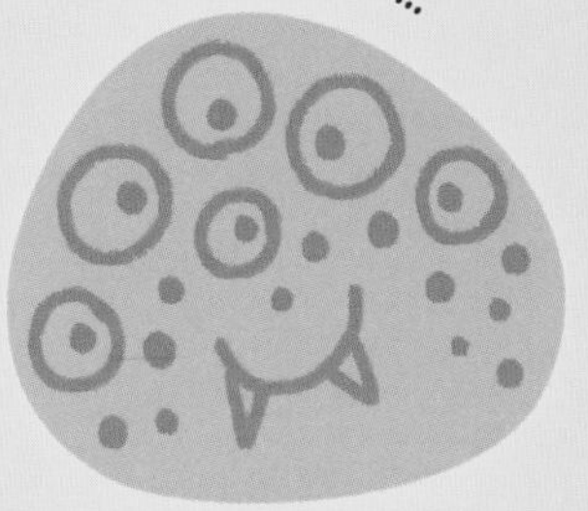

Turn these shapes into monster faces.

spots and stripes.

Ha ha ha....

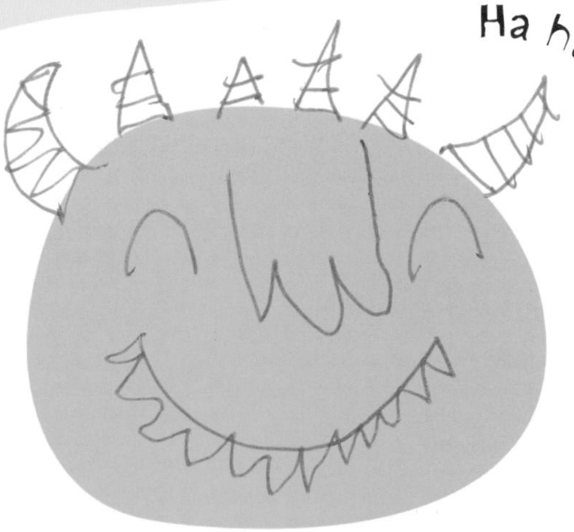

I'm a hairy monster.

I have three eyes.

I need some ears.

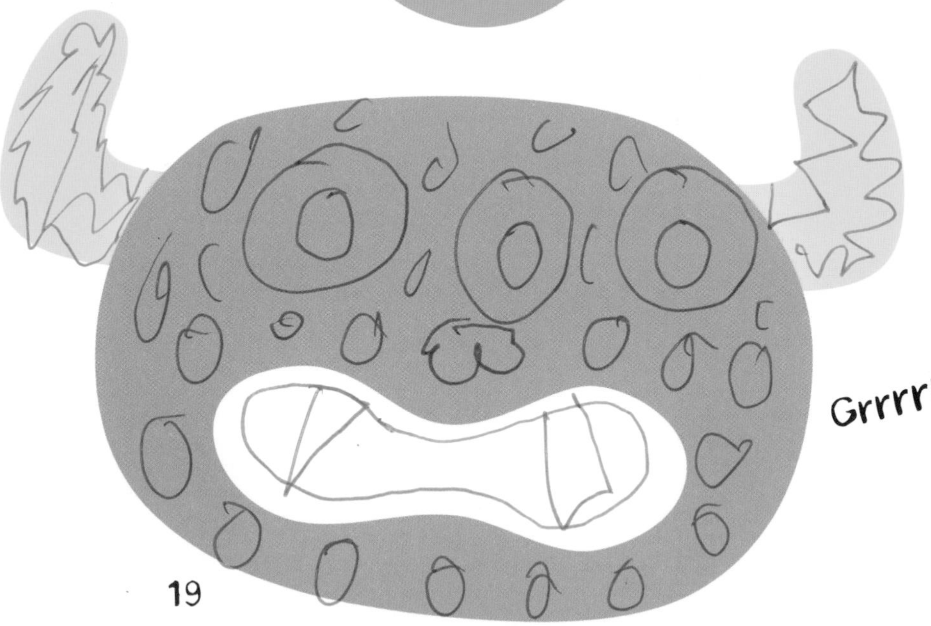

Grrrrrr!

Draw dolphins diving in the sea.

1 Draw a body...

2 a nose...

3 an eye and mouth.

Draw a fatter shape for a whale.

Sploosh!

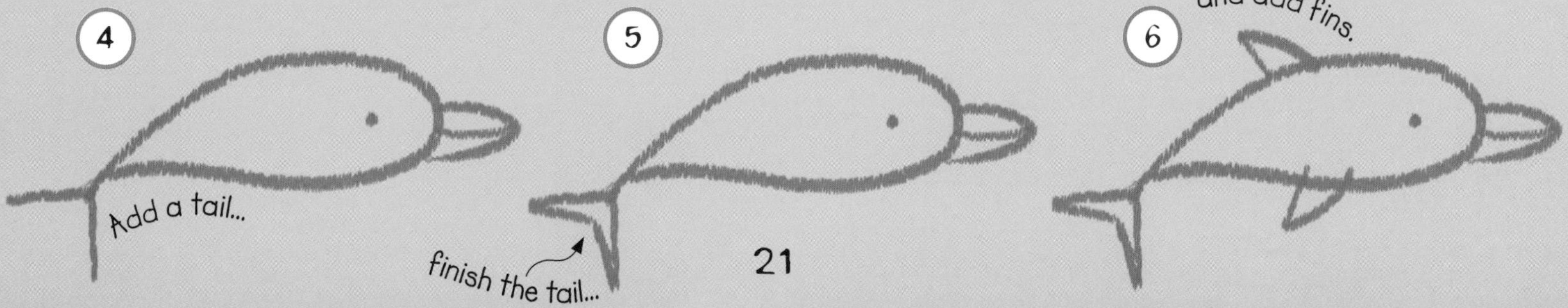
4
Add a tail...
5
finish the tail...
6
and add fins.

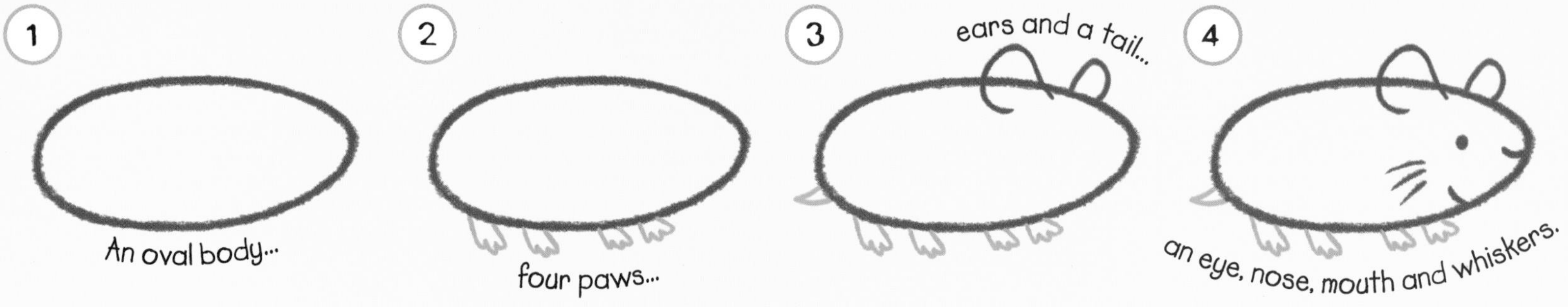
1
2
3
4
An oval body...
four paws...
ears and a tail...
an eye, nose, mouth and whiskers.

Draw hamsters in a cage.

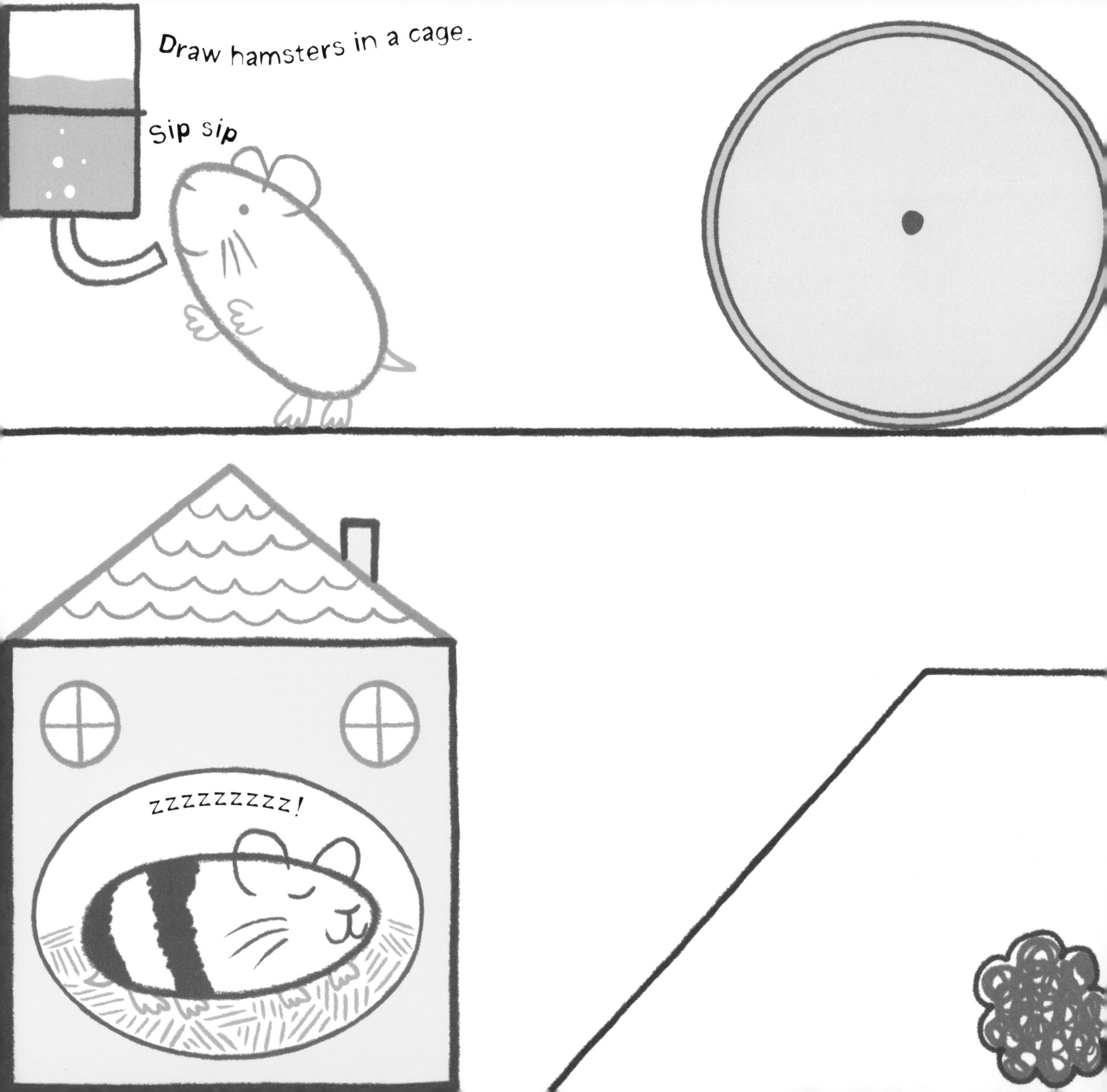
Sip sip
zzzzzzzzz!

1
An oval...
2
four paws...
3
ears and a tail...
4
an eye, nose, mouth and whiskers.

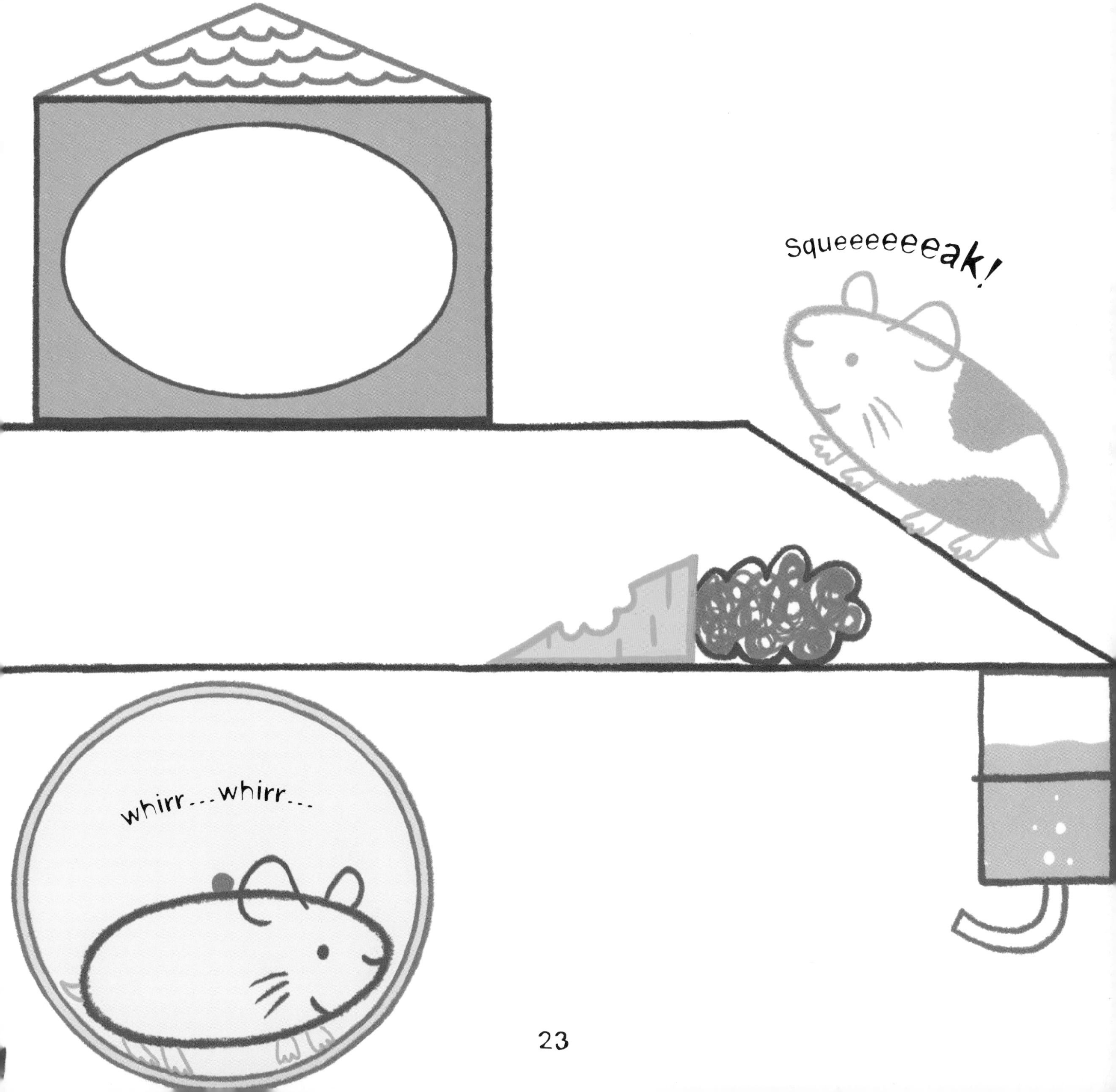
squeeeeeeeak!
whirr...whirr...

Draw dragonflies and flowers.

1

A body...

2

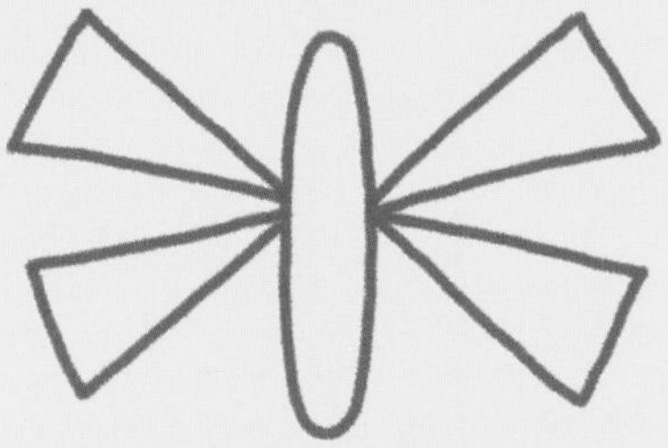

four wings...

3

eyes and stripes.

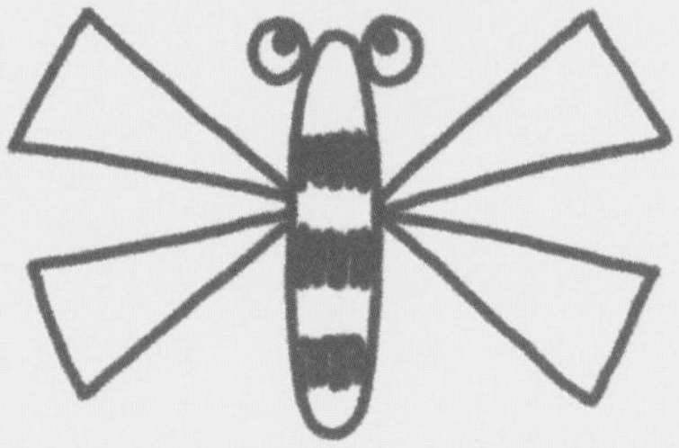

Bzzzzzzzzzzz

1
Flower petals...
2
lines and dots.

Draw cats on walls.

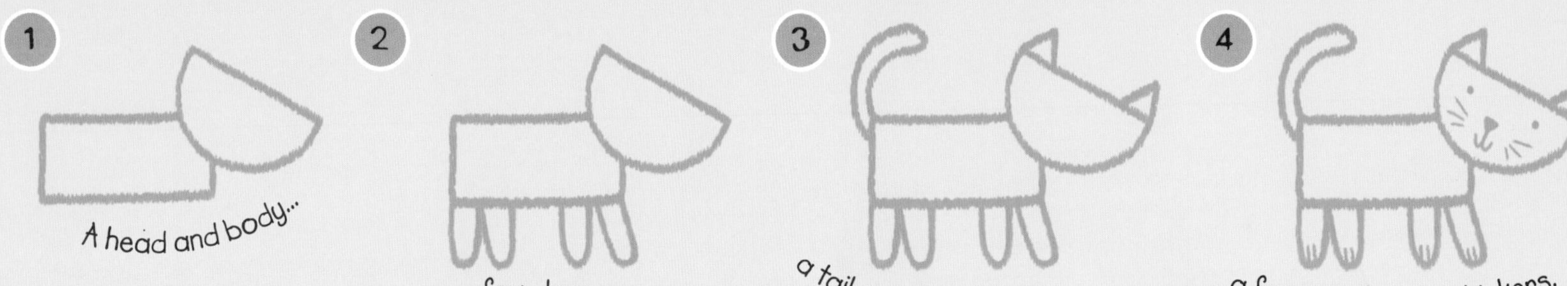

1 A head and body...

2 four legs...

3 a tail and two ears...

4 a face and some whiskers.

1 A head and body...

2 front legs...

3 a tail and two ears...

4 a face and some whiskers.

Snuffle

Draw hedgehogs and toadstools.

1
A curved top...
2
a fat stalk...
3
and lots of spots.

1

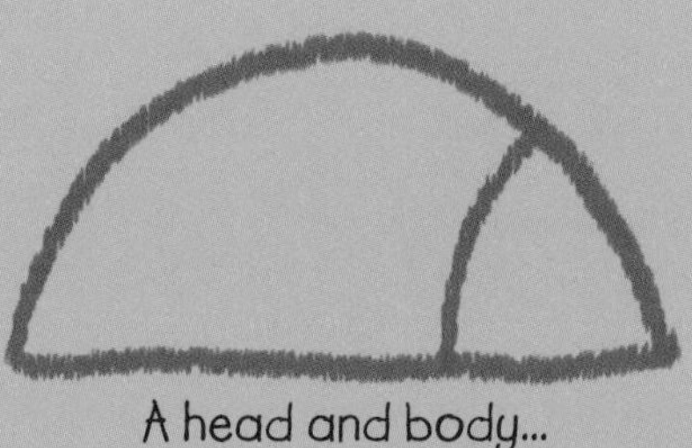

A head and body...

2

an eye, nose and mouth...

3

lots of spikes and feet.

1

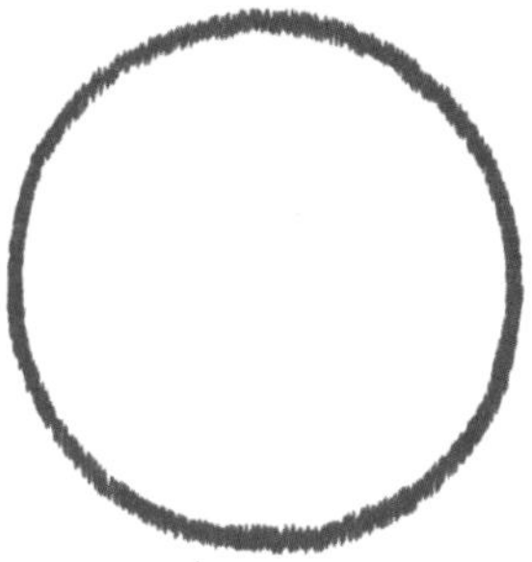

A circle...

2

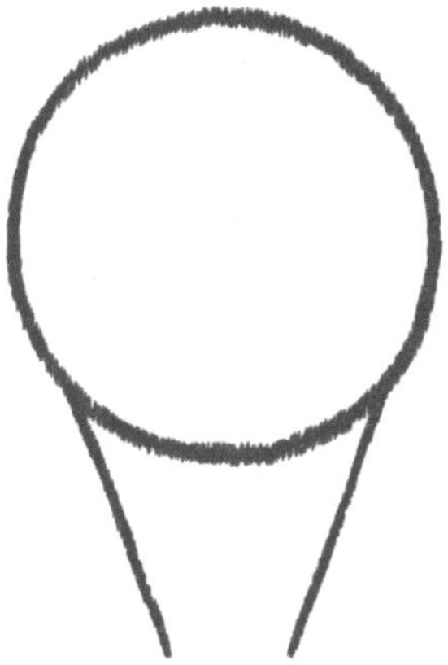

two lines...

3

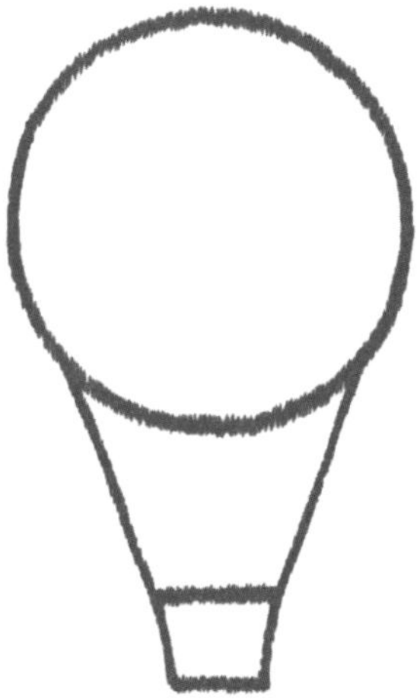

a basket...

4

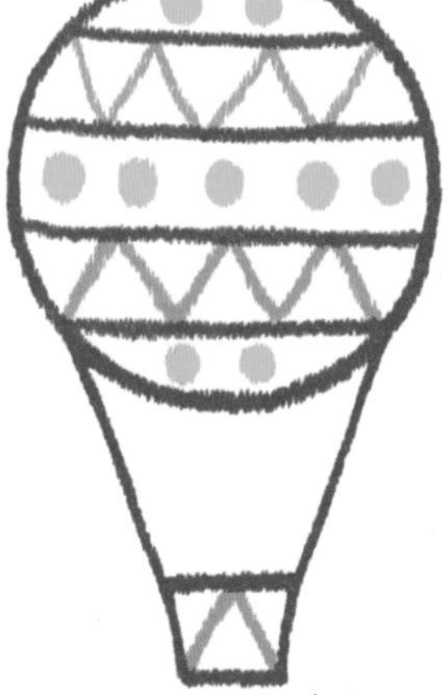

lines, spots and zigzags.

Draw hot-air balloons floating across the sky.

Turn this circle into a balloon.

1

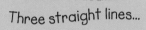

Three straight lines...

2

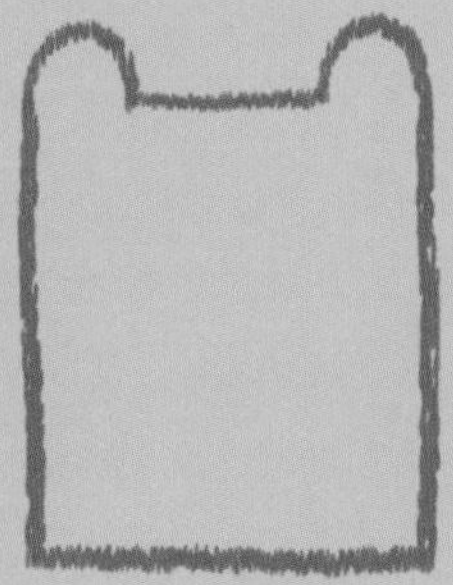

ears and the top of the head...

3

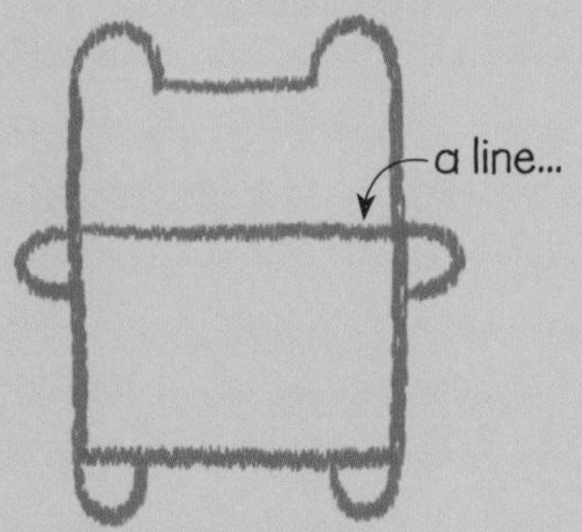
a line...

and four paws...

4

eyes, a nose and a mouth...

5

a tie and some stripes.

It's cold!

Draw bears in the woods.

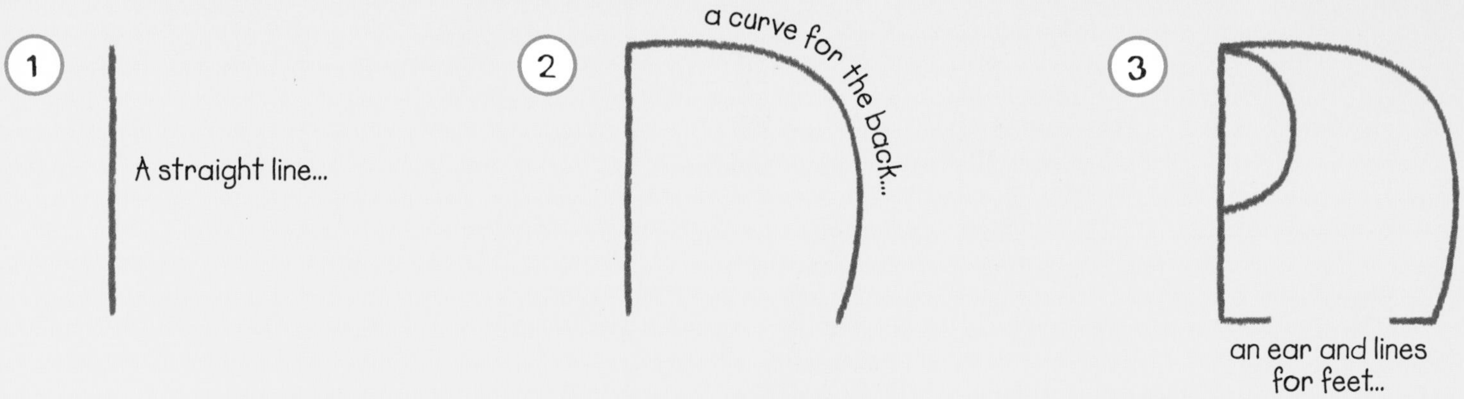
1
A straight line...
2
a curve for the back...
3
an ear and lines for feet...

Draw big and little elephants.

Splooooosh!

4
another small curve...
5
a head and trunk...
6
an eye, tusk and tail.

Please decorate my blanket.

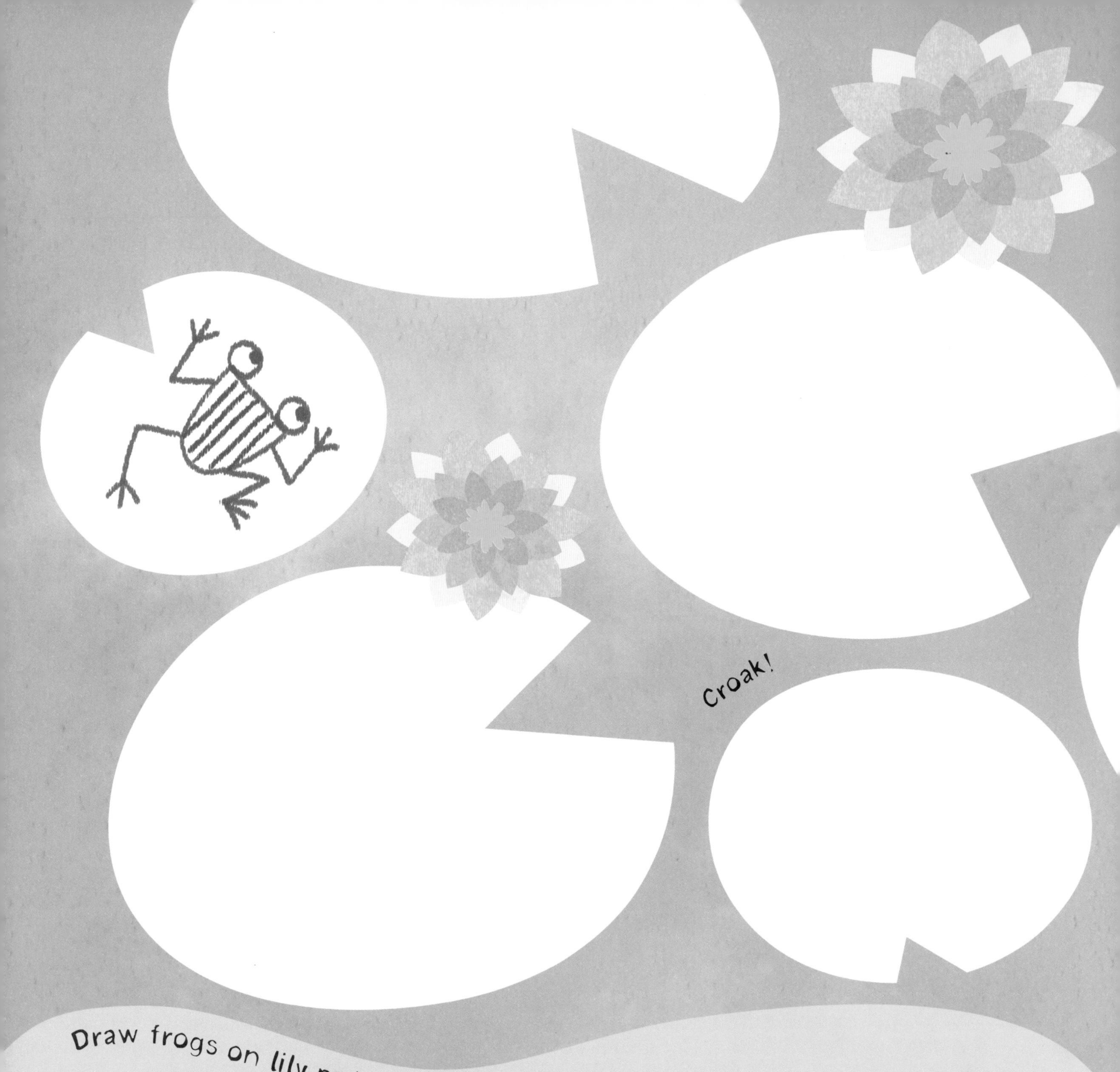
Croak!

Draw frogs on lily pads.

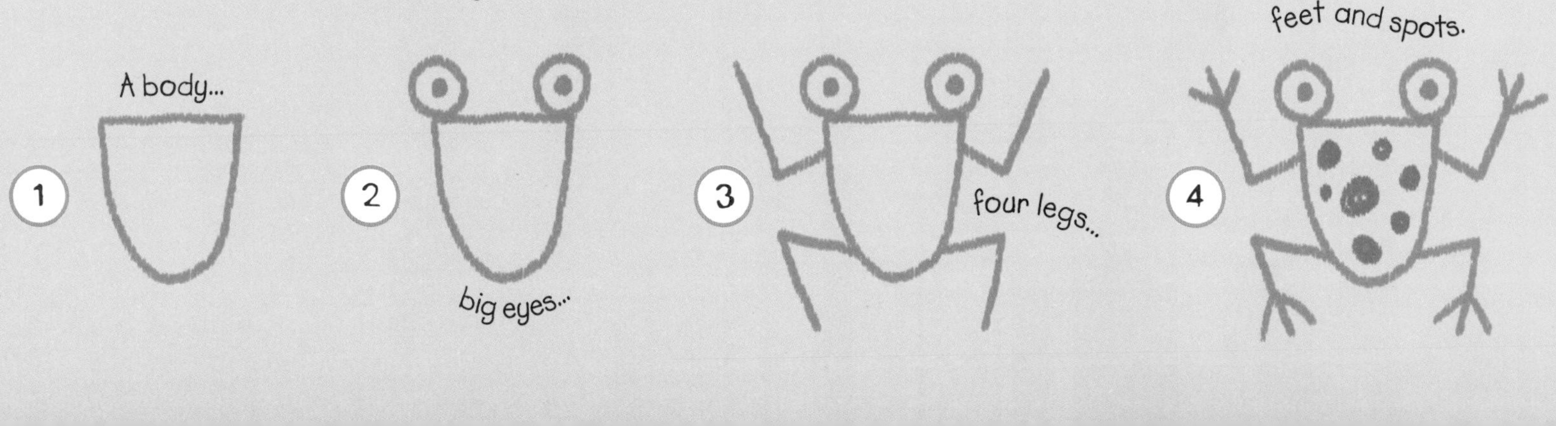
1
A body...
2
big eyes...
3
four legs...
4
feet and spots.

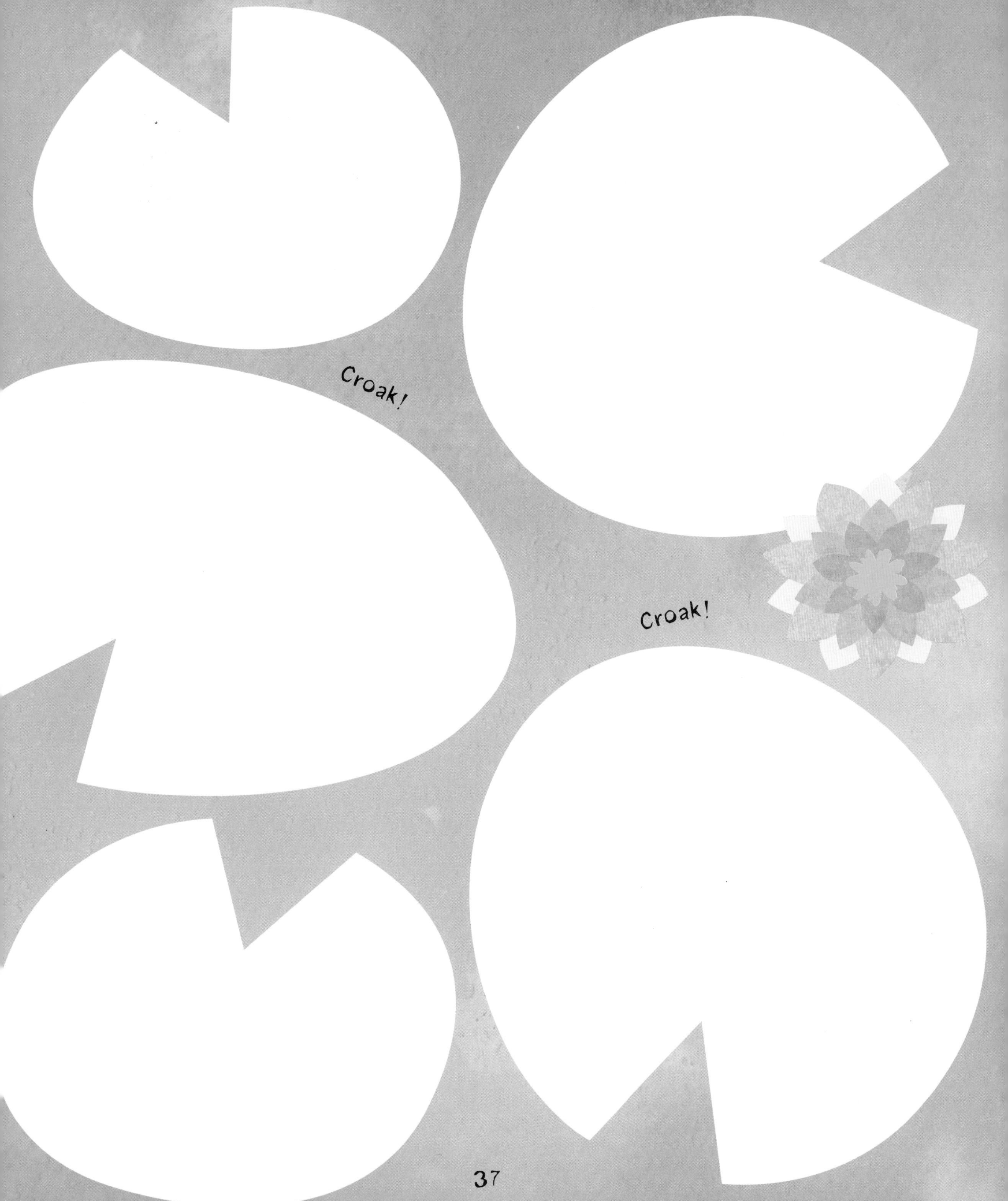
Croak!
Croak!

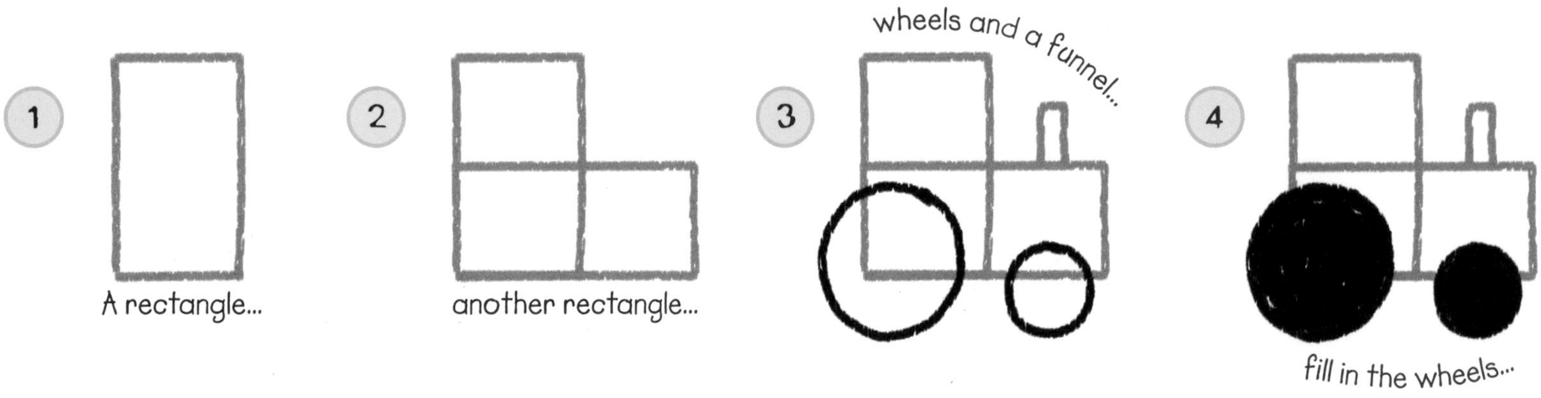
1
A rectangle...
2
another rectangle...
3
wheels and a funnel...
4
fill in the wheels...

Draw tractors and sheep in the fields.
Baaaa

5

add a trailer...

6

and fill it with hay.

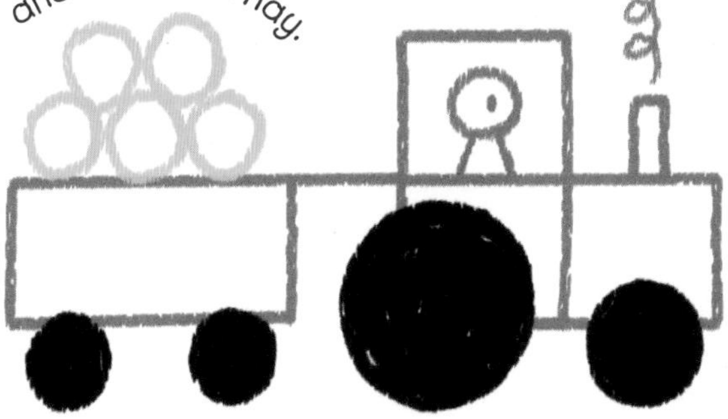

Draw muddy pigs.

1

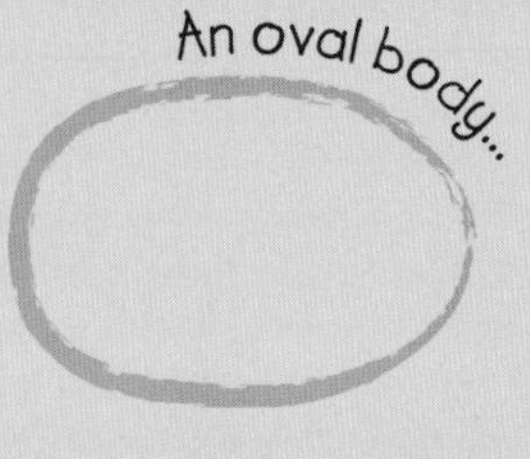
An oval body...

2

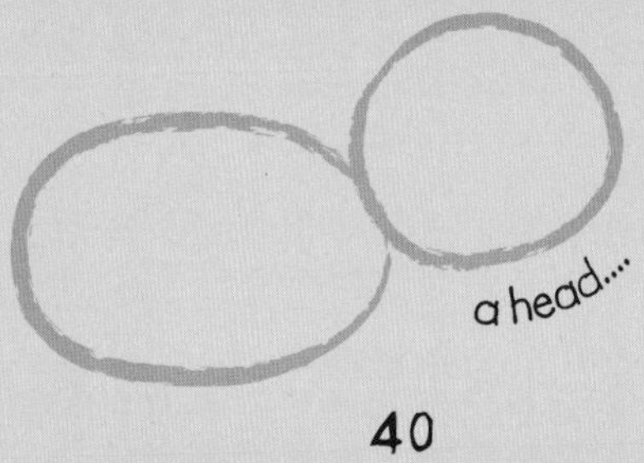
a head...

3

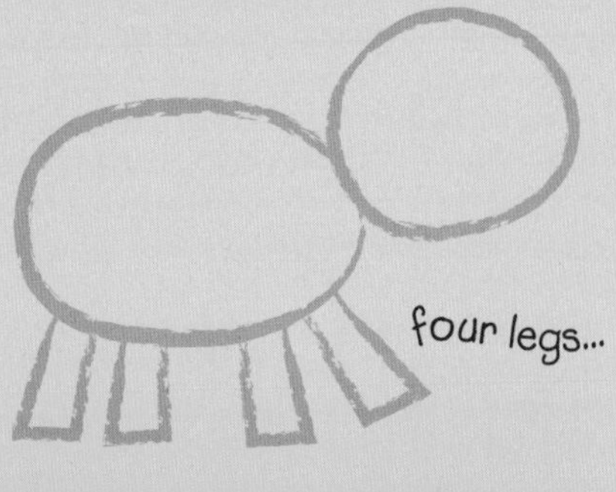
four legs...

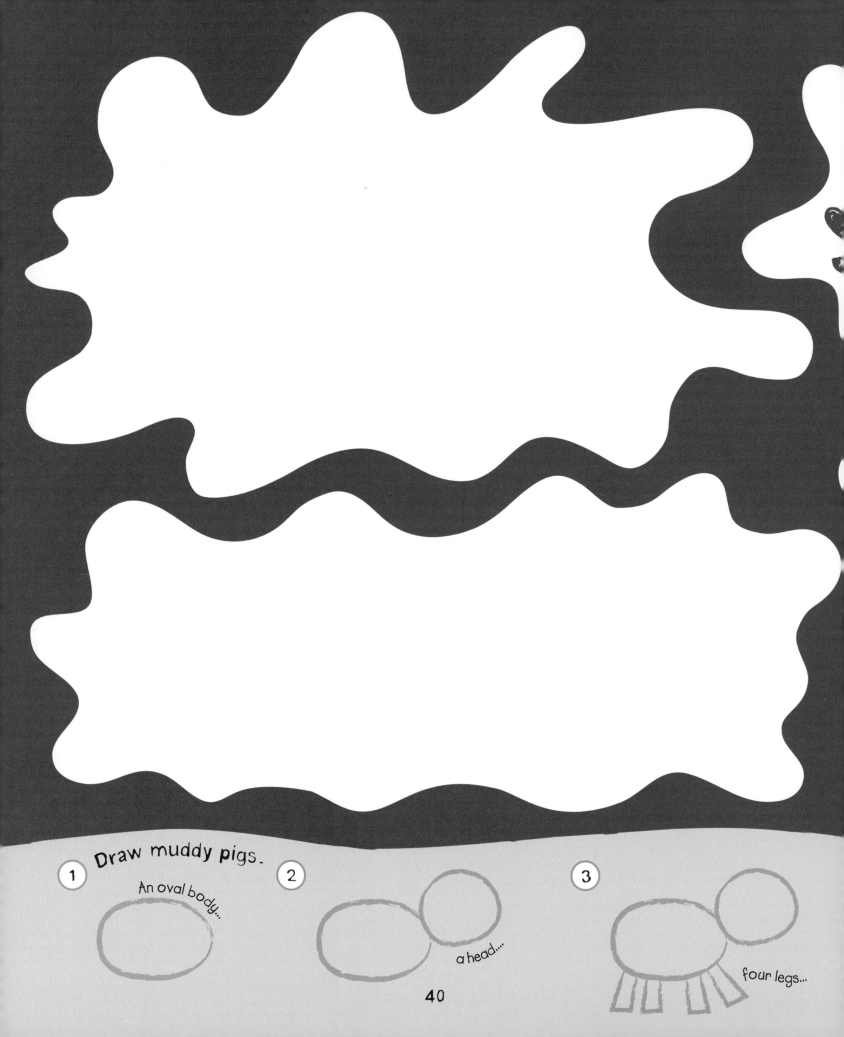

4
two ears...
5
fill in the ears...
draw a nose...
6
add eyes, a mouth and a curly tail.

Draw climbing koalas...

1
An oval body...
2
ears...
3
an arm and paw...
4
a leg and foot...
5
eyes and a nose.

Zzzzzzzzz

...and pandas.

Round ears...

1

panda eyes...

2

...black and white.

3

This lonely panda wants some friends.

Draw robots...robots...robots.

A head and body...

1

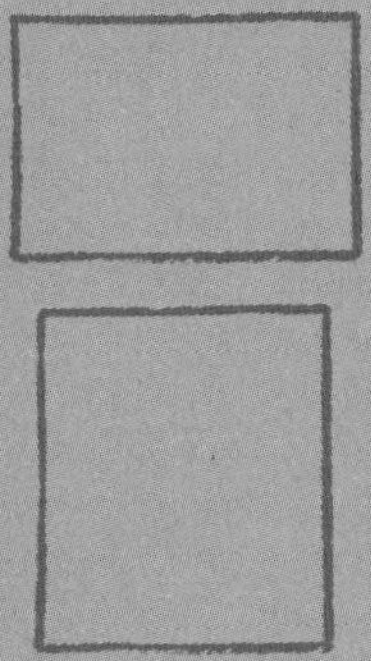

a neck, legs and feet...

2

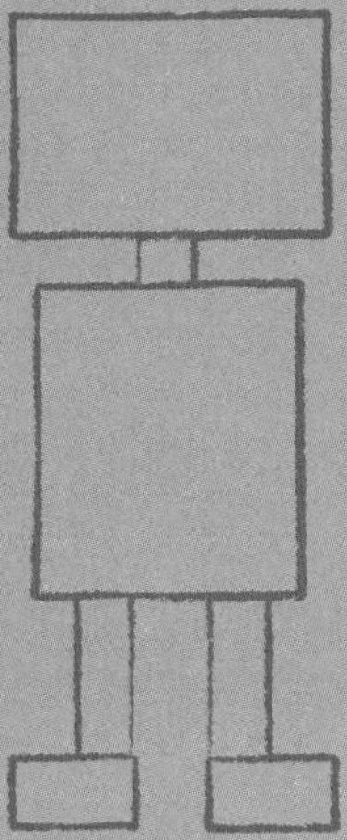

arms and hands.

3

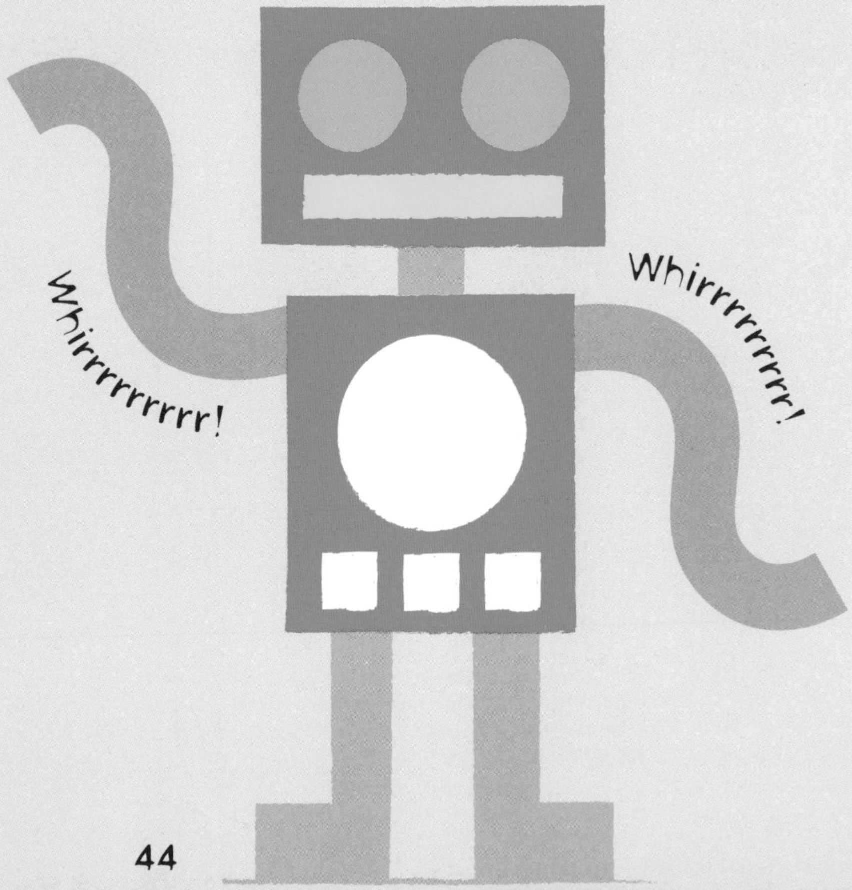
Whirrrrrrrrr!
Whirrrrrrrrr!

Add ears and a tummy...

4

big eyes and a mouth...

5

stripes and an antenna.

6

1
A head and body...
2
an eye and a beak...
3
legs and a wing...
4
and little feet.

Draw ducks on the riverbanks.

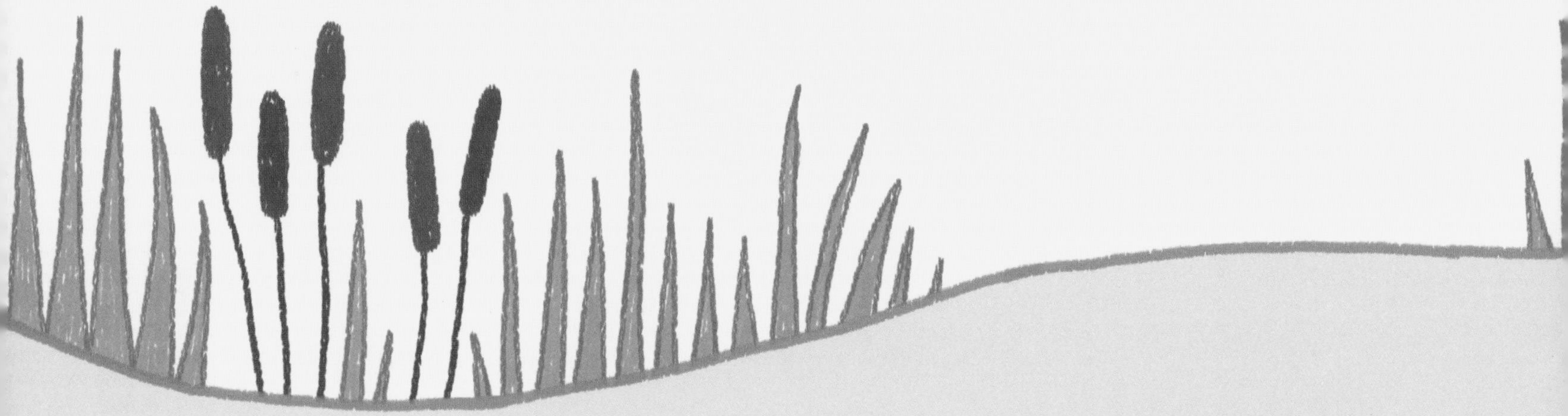

Quack...quack...quack

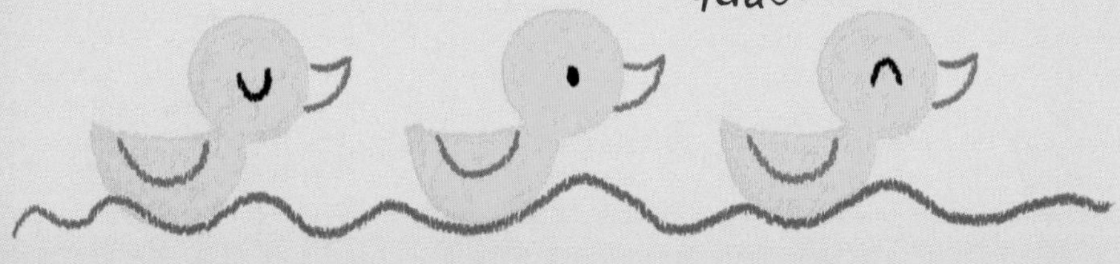

Draw some more swimming ducks, like me.

eyebrows?
glasses?
eyelashes?
surprised eyes?
Choose some eyes...
Draw lots of faces.

tied up?
curly?
straight?
and a hairstyle...
and a mouth.
small lips?
smiling?
yawning or singing?

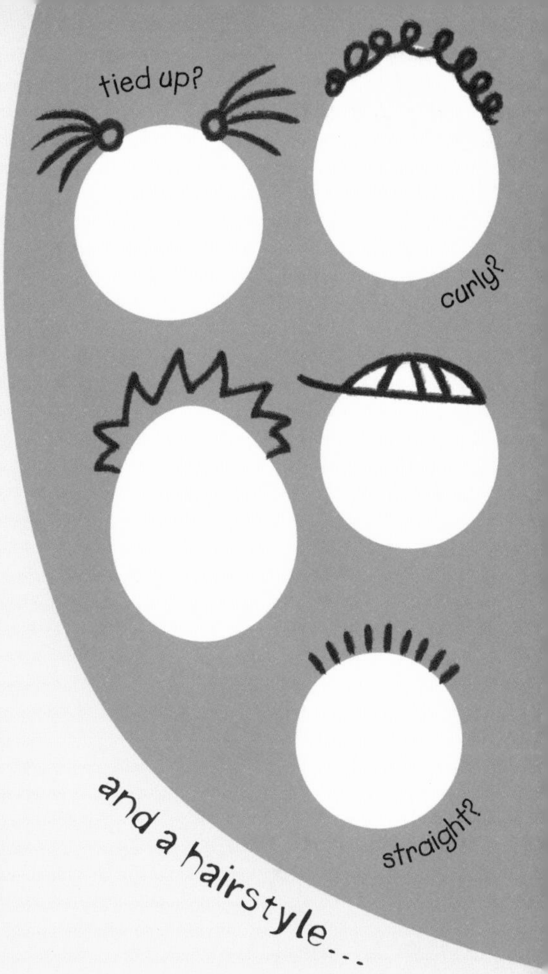

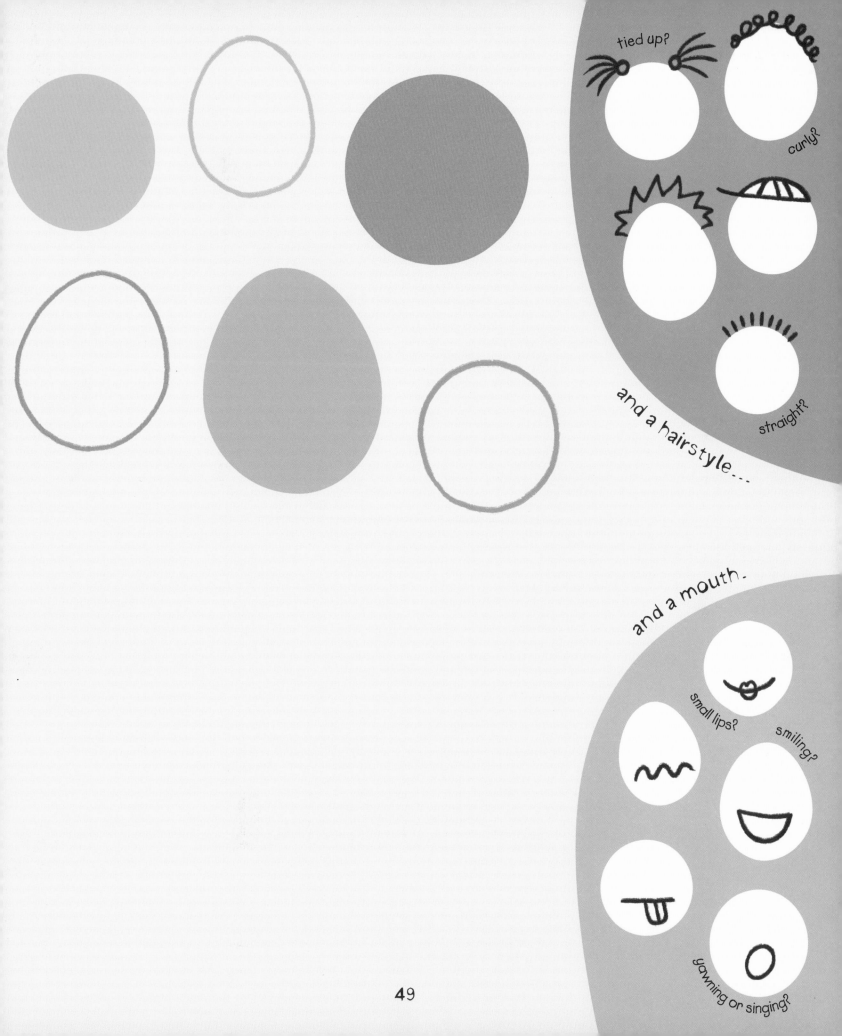

Draw aliens in space.

1

An oval spacecraft...

2

a head and body...

3

arms and hands...

4

two antennae...

5

and a face.

Draw rabbits in a vegetable patch.

1
A head and body...
2
ears and a tail...
3
eyes, a nose, mouth
and whiskers.

1
A head and body...
2
ears and a tail...
3
eyes, a nose, mouth
and whiskers.

I'm
hungr

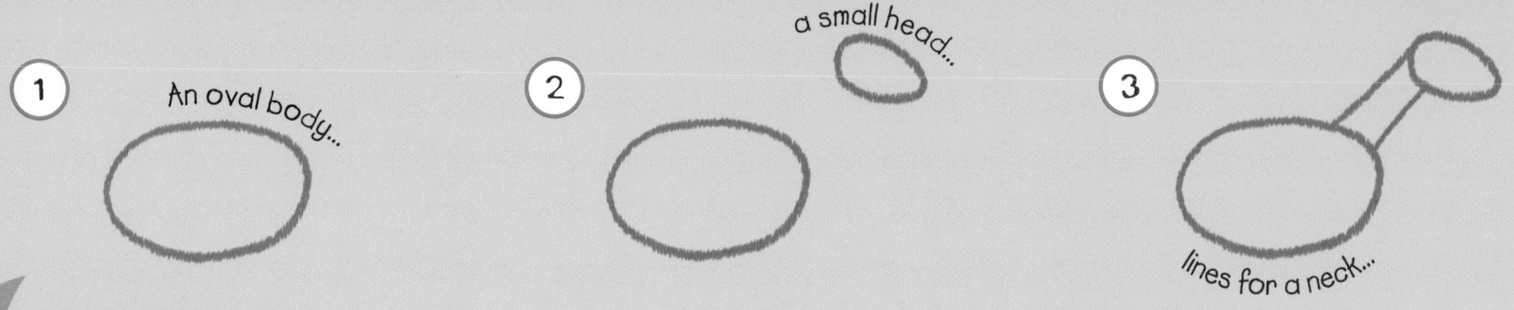
1
An oval body...
2
a small head...
3
lines for a neck...

Draw hungry dinosaurs.

Chomp!
chomp!

4
four stumpy legs...
5
a long tail...
6
and lots of spikes.

Try big eyes...
straight legs....
curly wings...
claws....
open beak...
Hooot!
wings that stick out...

Turn these shapes into owls in a tree.

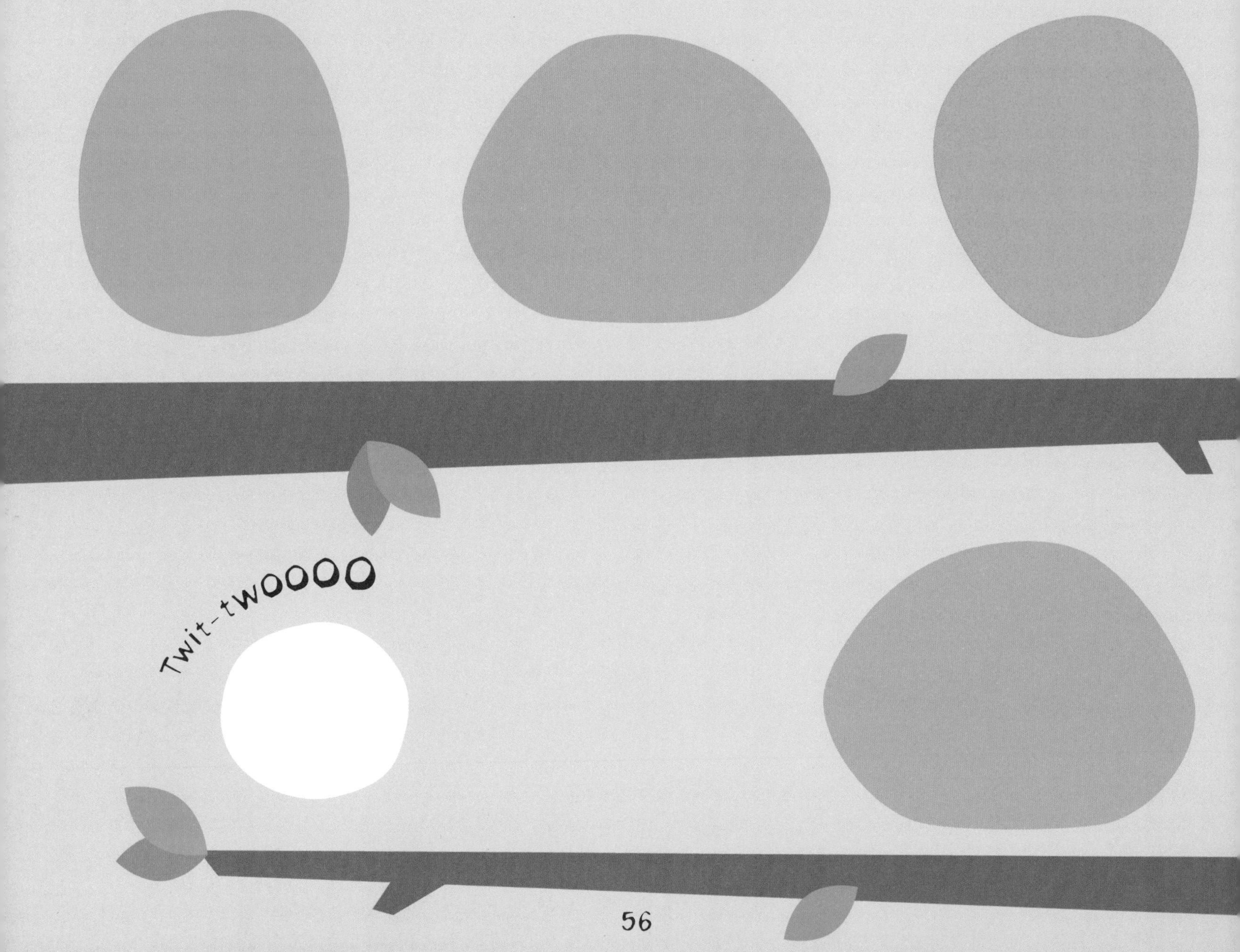
Twit-twOOOO

Hoo-hOOOO
I'm half asleep.

1

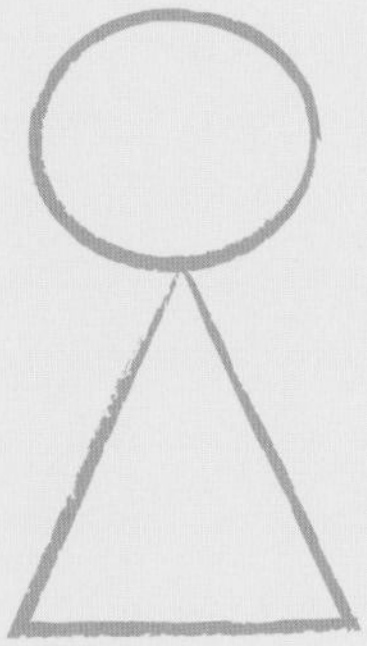

A head and triangle
for a dress...

2

four wings...

3

arms and legs...

Draw fairies flying around the flowers.

I'd like a wand.

add hair...

4

hands and feet...

5

eyes and a smile.

6

Draw ships sailing on the sea.

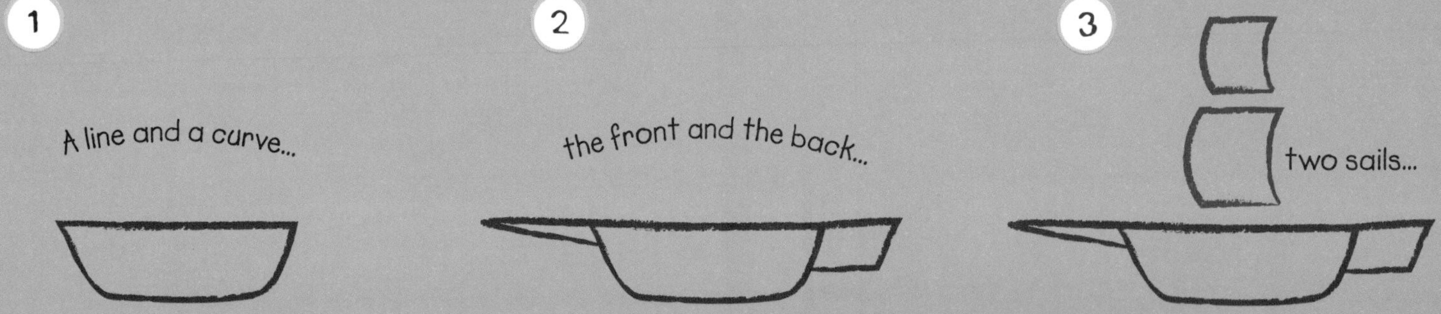
1
A line and a curve...
2
the front and the back...
3
two sails...

4
two more sails...
5
lines for the masts...
6
...and add flags.

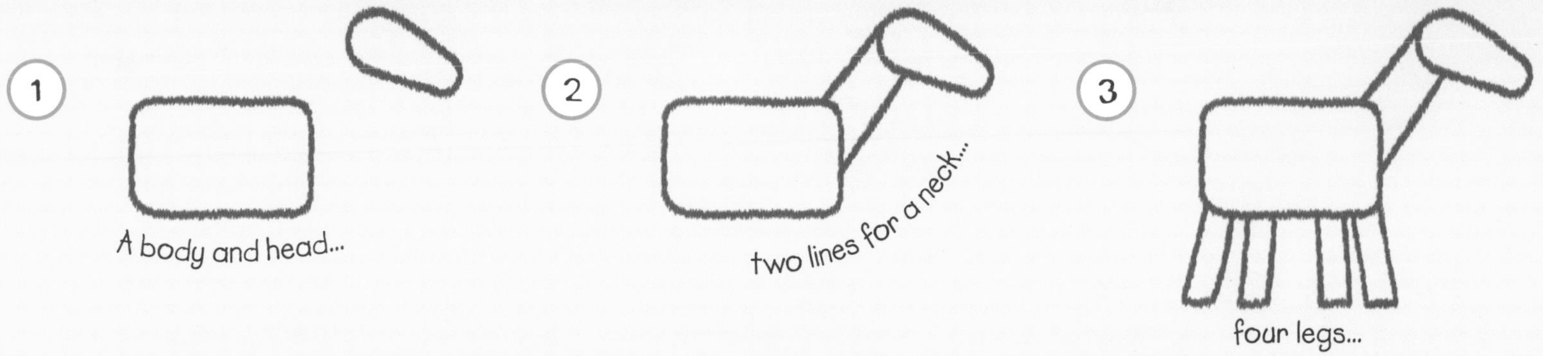
1
A body and head...
2
two lines for a neck...
3
four legs...

Draw horses in the fields.

Neigh!

4
ears and an eye...
a nose and mouth...
hooves...

5
a mane and a tail...

6
spots on the body...
and fill in the hooves.

Chomp...chomp...

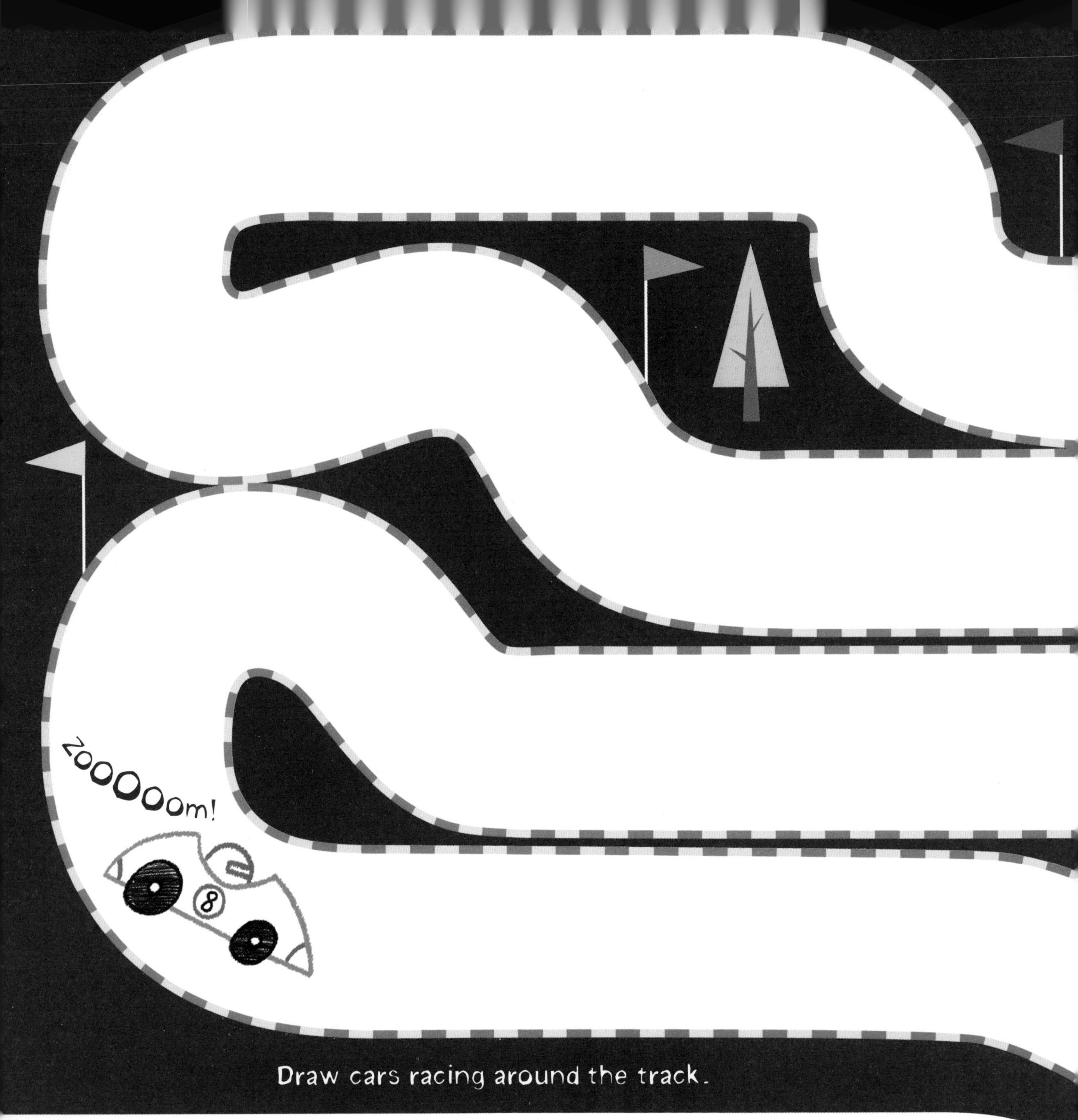

Draw cars racing around the track.

1

Draw this shape...

2

two wheels...

3

fill in the wheels...

4

and add a driver and stripes.

Be careful at the corner.
vroOOOOom!
The finish line!

1
A head with ears...
2
a curly mane...
3
a body...

Draw lions hiding the grass.

I'm a lioness.
I don't have a mane.

4
four legs...
5
eyes and a nose...
6
and a tail.

ZZZZZZ

Draw windmills and tulips.

1
A triangle...
2
two sails...
3
two more...
4
stripes...
5
...windows and a door.

1
A curve and a stalk...
2
a zigzag...
3
and leaves.

Draw penguins on the ice and swimming in the sea.

splosh!

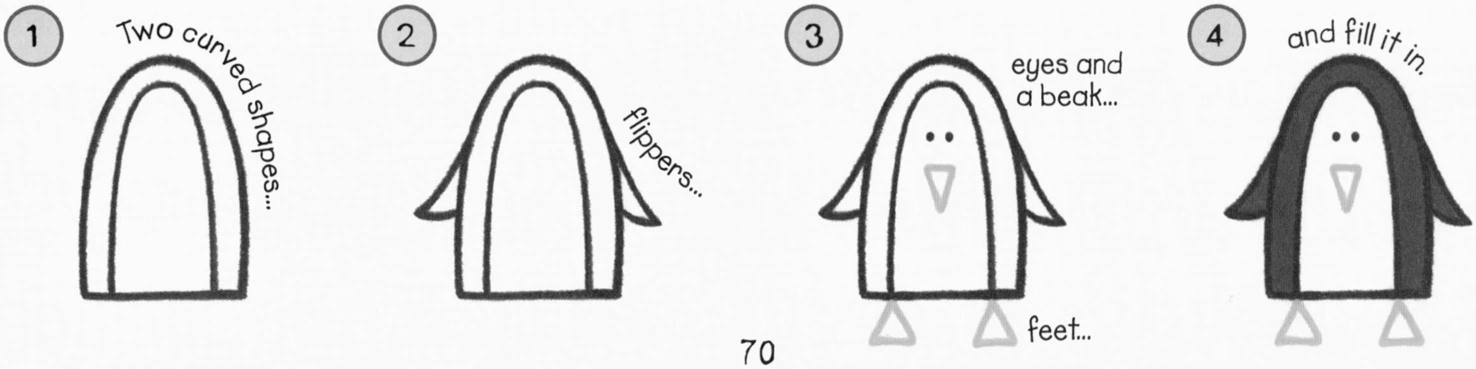

1
Two curved shapes...
2
flippers...
3
eyes and a beak...
feet...
4
and fill it in.

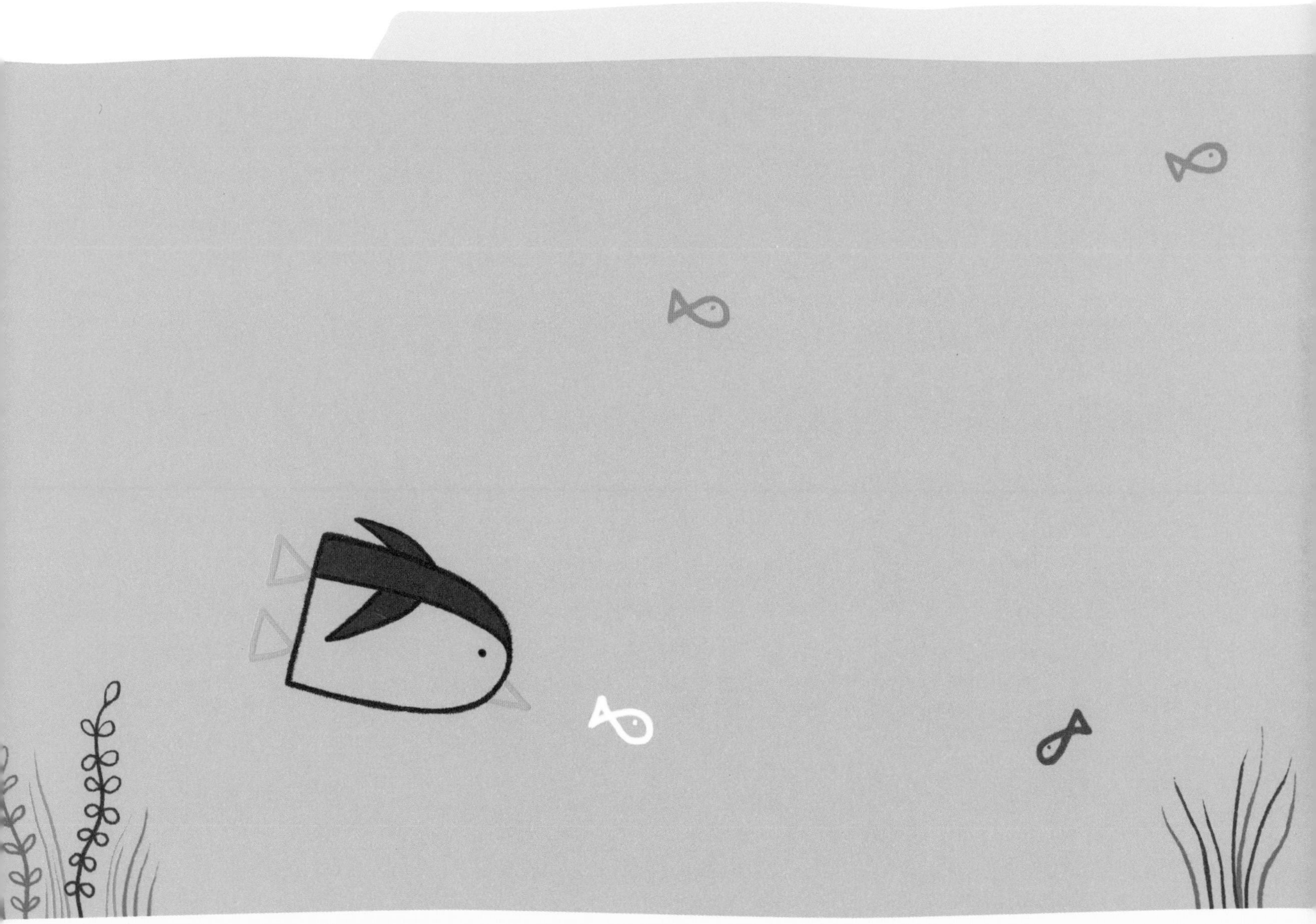

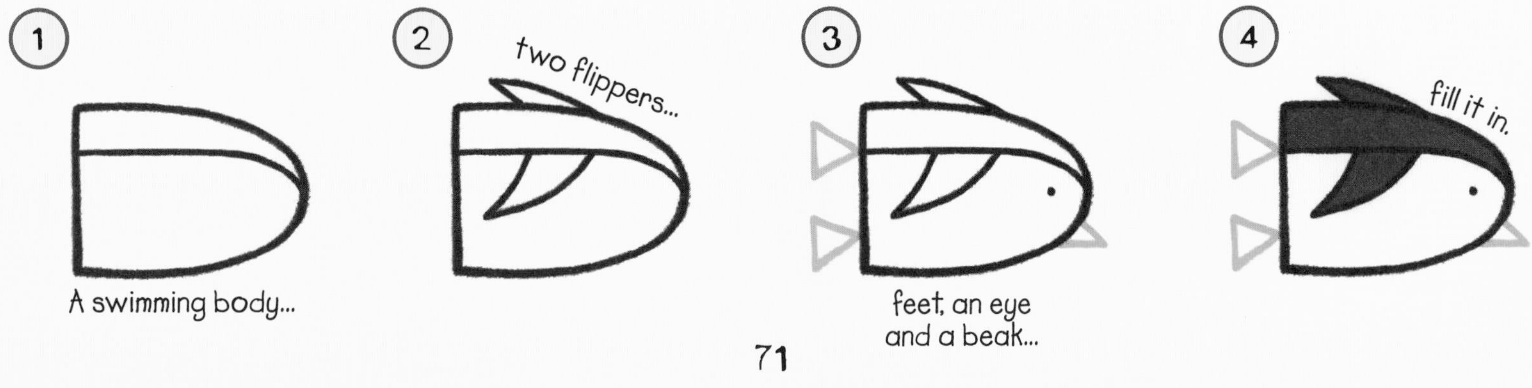

1
A swimming body...
2
two flippers...
3
feet, an eye
and a beak...
4
fill it in.

1 A head and neck...

2 top of the body...

3

a big skirt...

4 add hair...

Draw princesses in a palace garden.

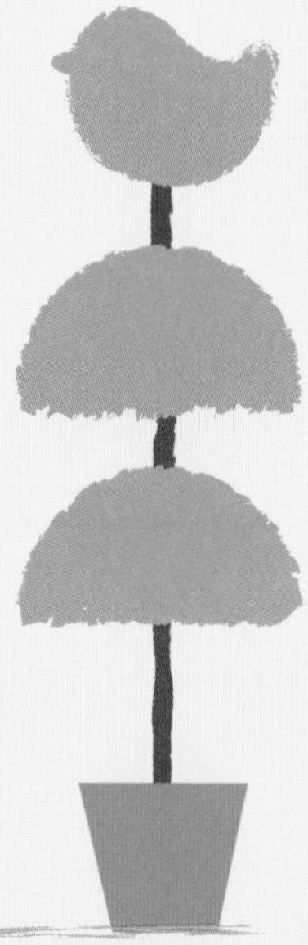

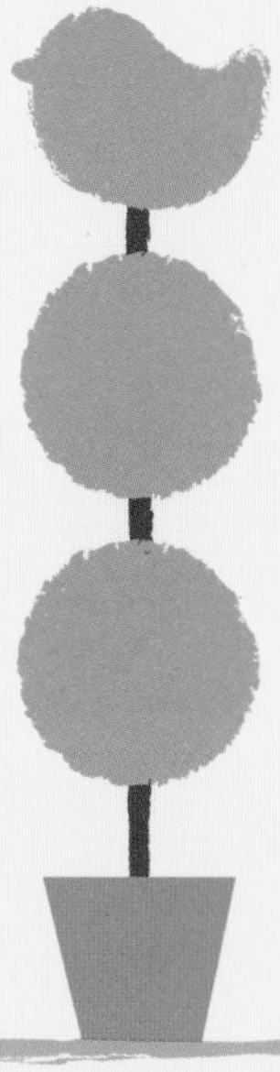

5 sleeves and arms...

hands and a crown...

6

eyes and a smile.

7

Draw dragons in Dragonland.

Whoosh!

1
A head and a body...
2
lines for a neck and wings...
3
a tail...
and finish the wings.

4 Add four legs...

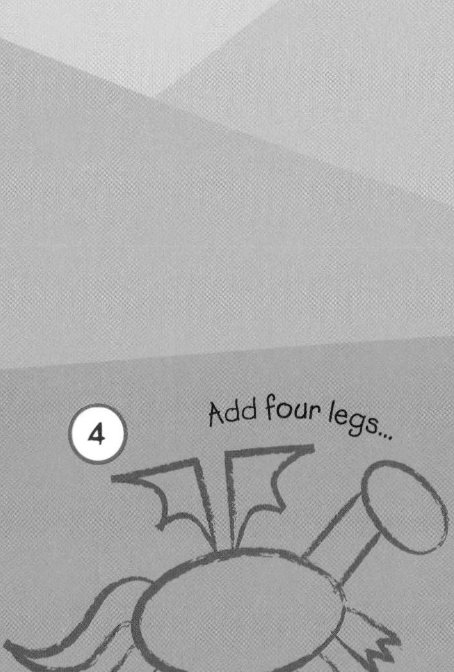

5 ears and a triangle on the tail...

6

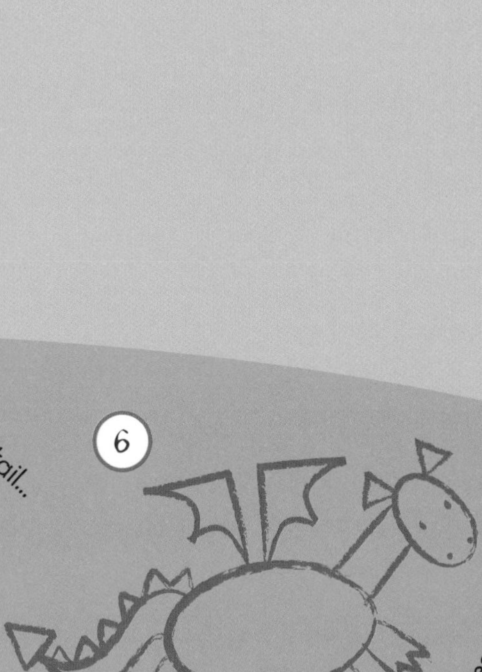

eyes, nostrils and spikes.

1
A rectangle...
2
a curved roof...
3
two lines for windows...
4
two wheels...
5
and a curly line.

Draw trucks, cars and houses.

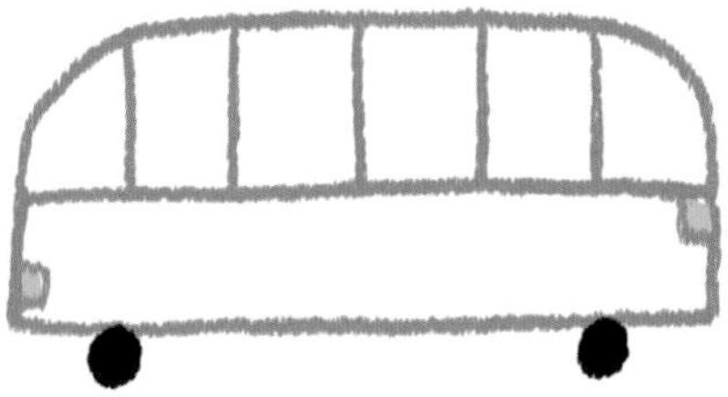

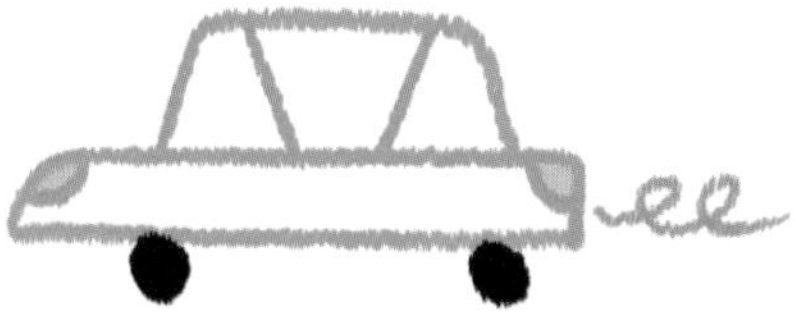

1

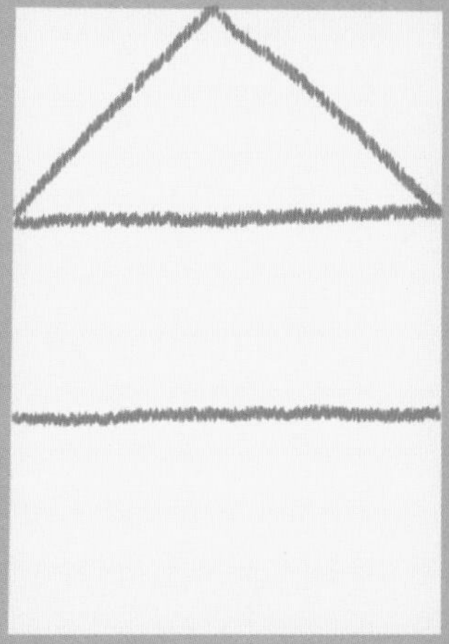

A triangle and a line...

2

a chimney, windows and a door...

some smoke...

3

roof tiles and window panes.

Draw planes in the sky...

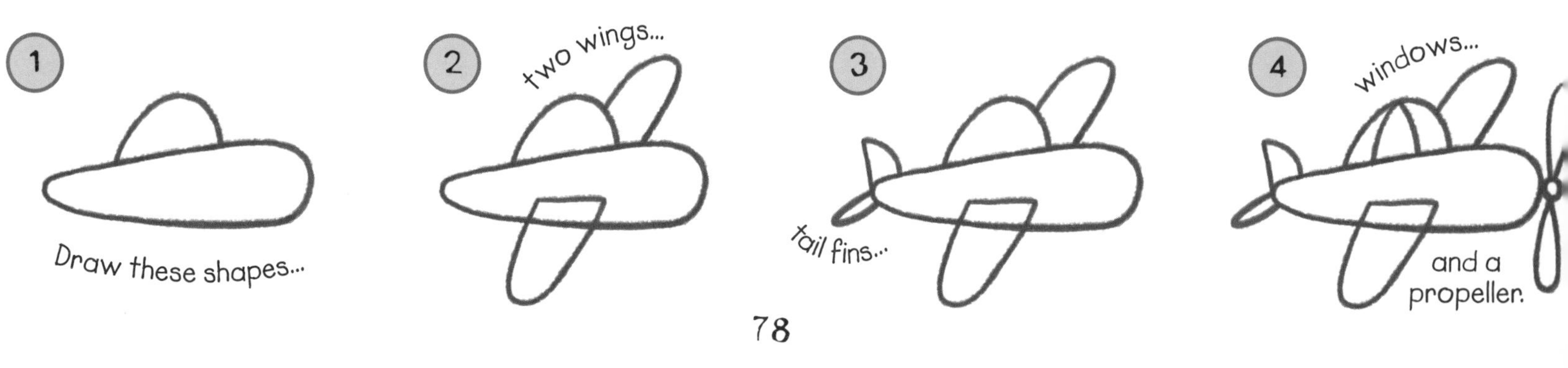

1
Draw these shapes...
2
two wings...
3
tail fins...
4
windows...
and a propeller.

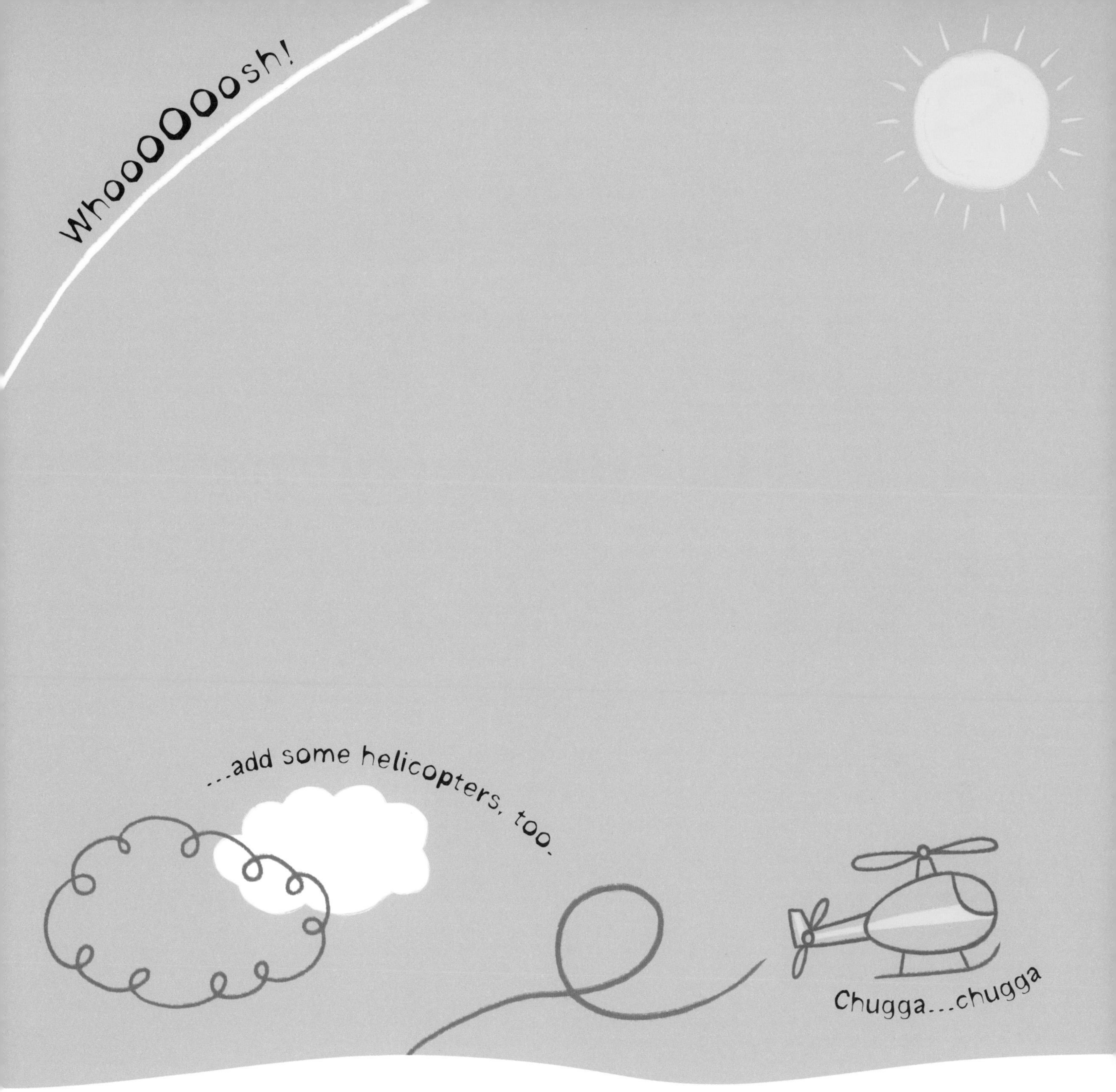
WhooOOOosh!
...add some helicopters, too.
Chugga...chugga

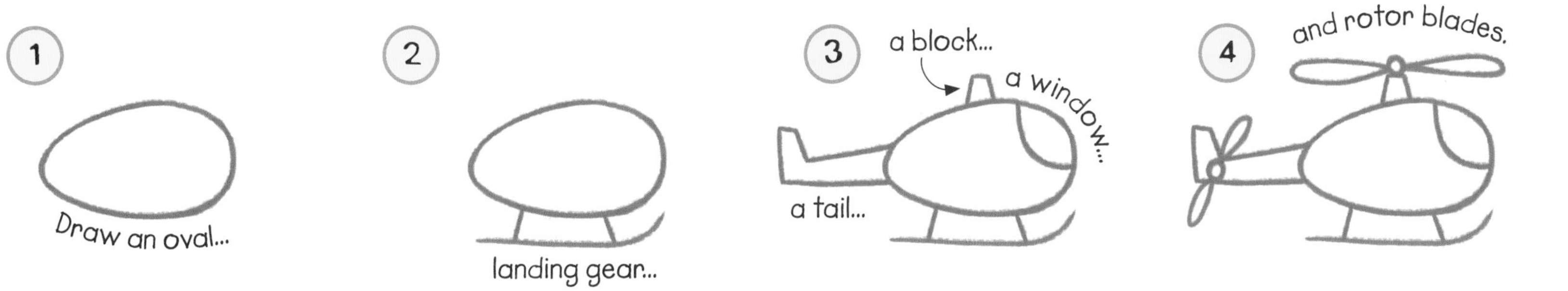
1
Draw an oval...
2
landing gear...
3
a block...
a window...
a tail...
4
and rotor blades.

1

A head and body...

2

a long tail...

3

four legs...

4

bumps on the back and head...

5

eyes, nostrils and sharp teeth.

Draw crocodiles in the swamp.

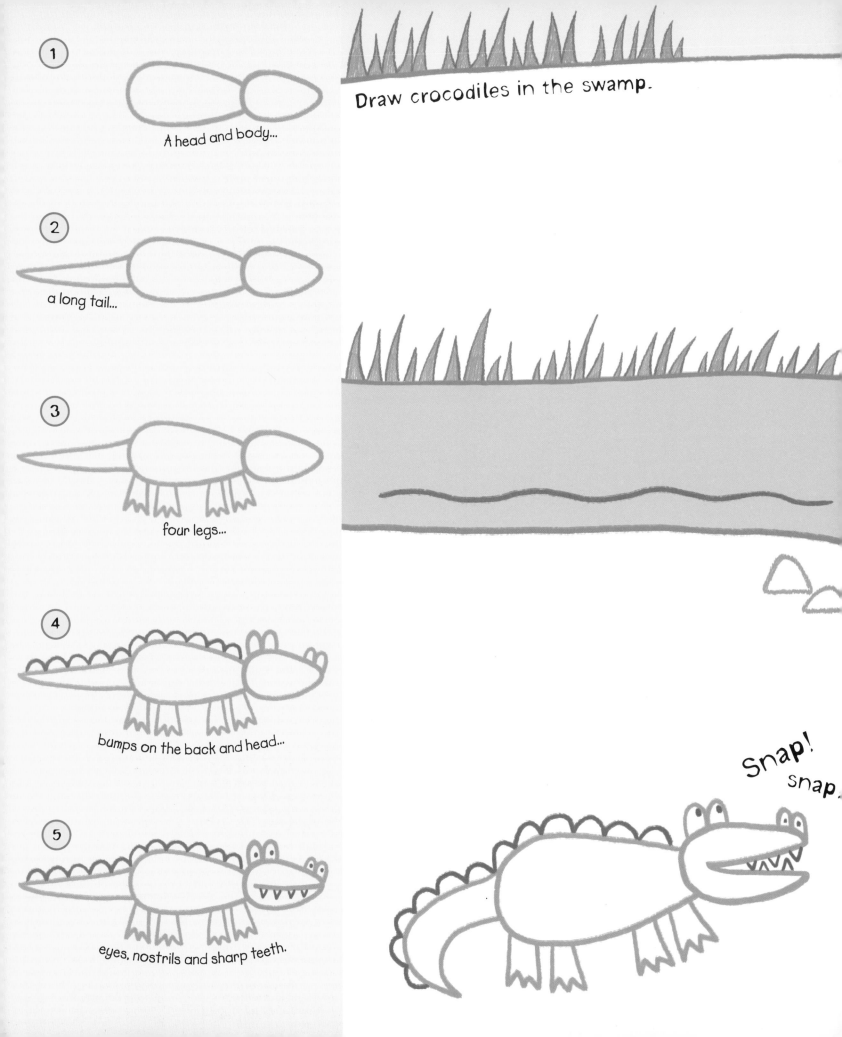

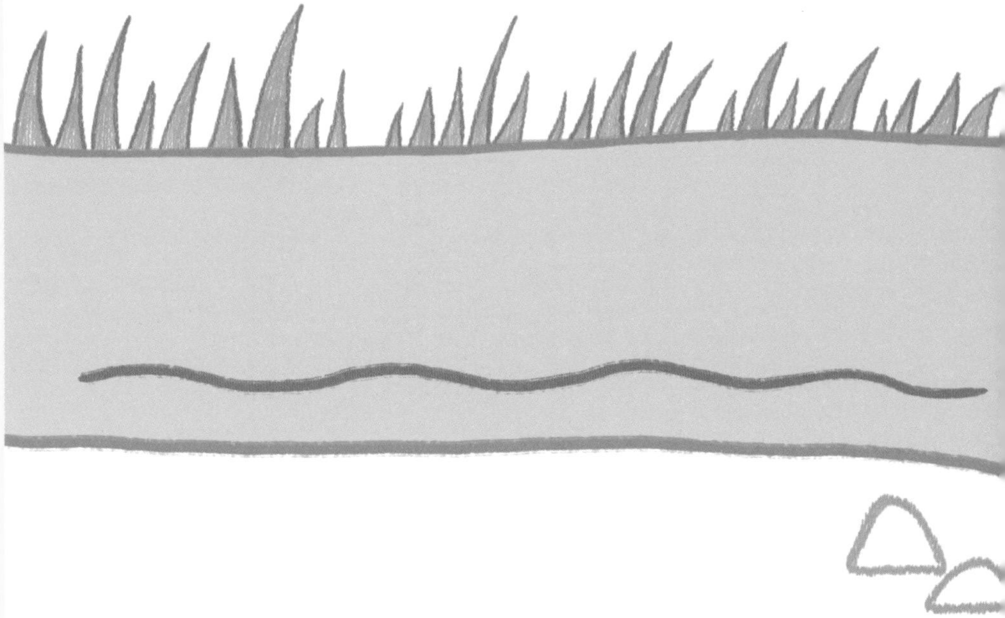

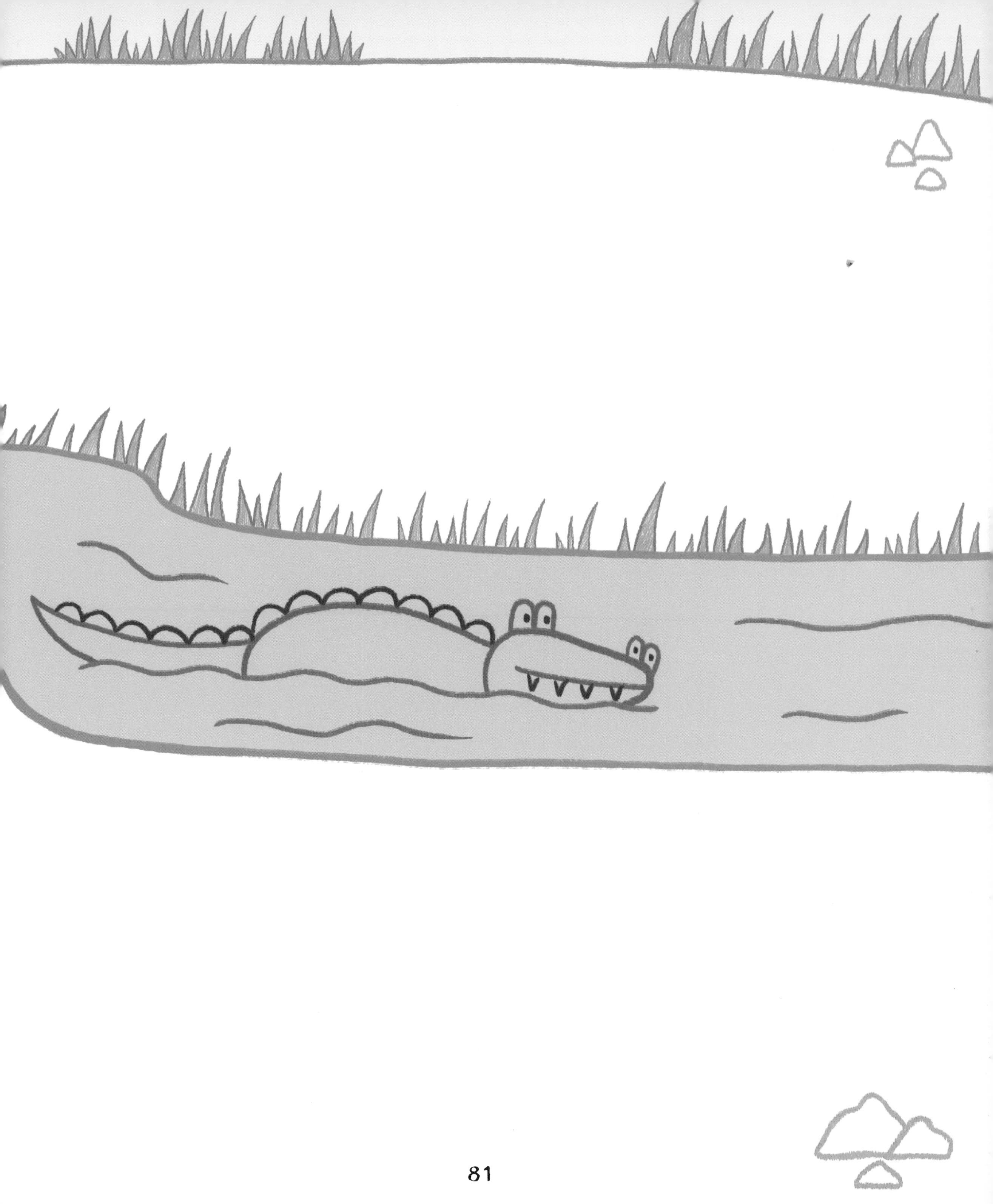

Draw diggers on the building site.

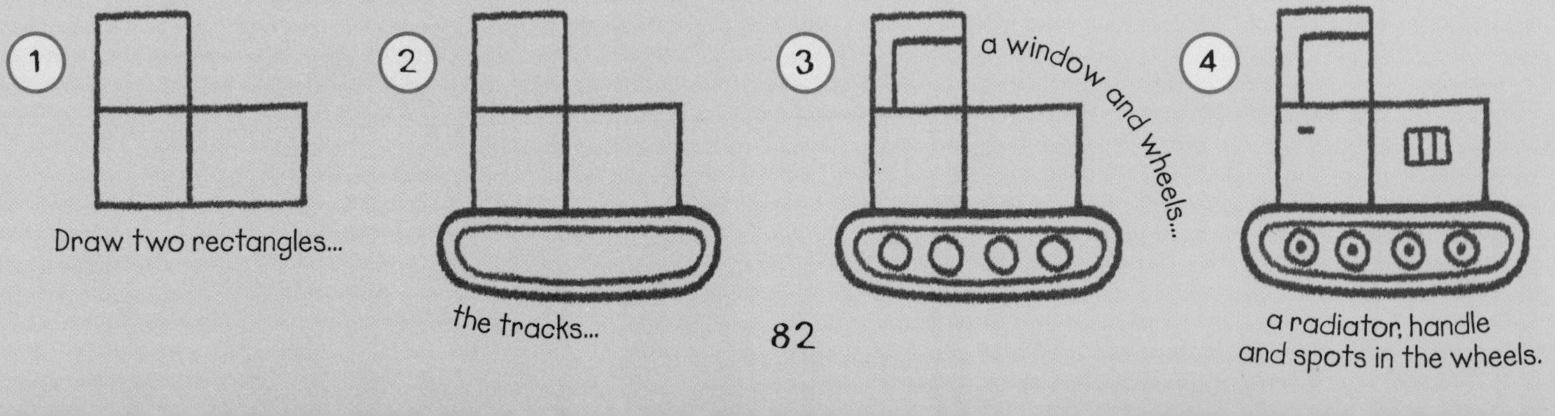

1
Draw two rectangles...
2
the tracks...
3
a window and wheels...
4
a radiator, handle and spots in the wheels.

Chug...chug!
Draw more rocks to be lifted.
Tools to attach
an excavator
a lifter
a grabber

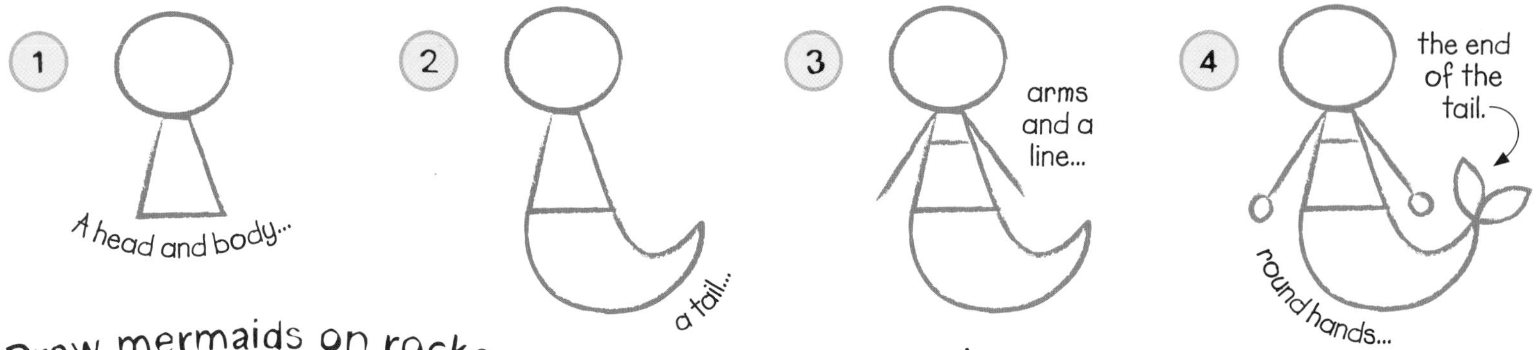
1
A head and body...
2
a tail...
3
arms and a line...
4
the end of the tail.
round hands...

Draw mermaids on rocks or swimming in the **pool**.

5

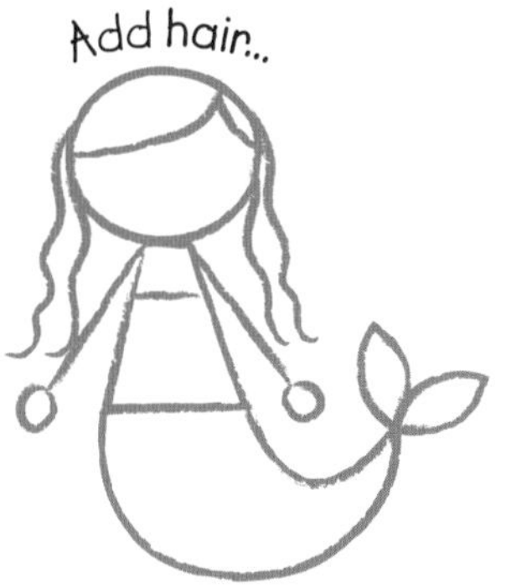
Add hair...

6

a face...
and wavy scales.

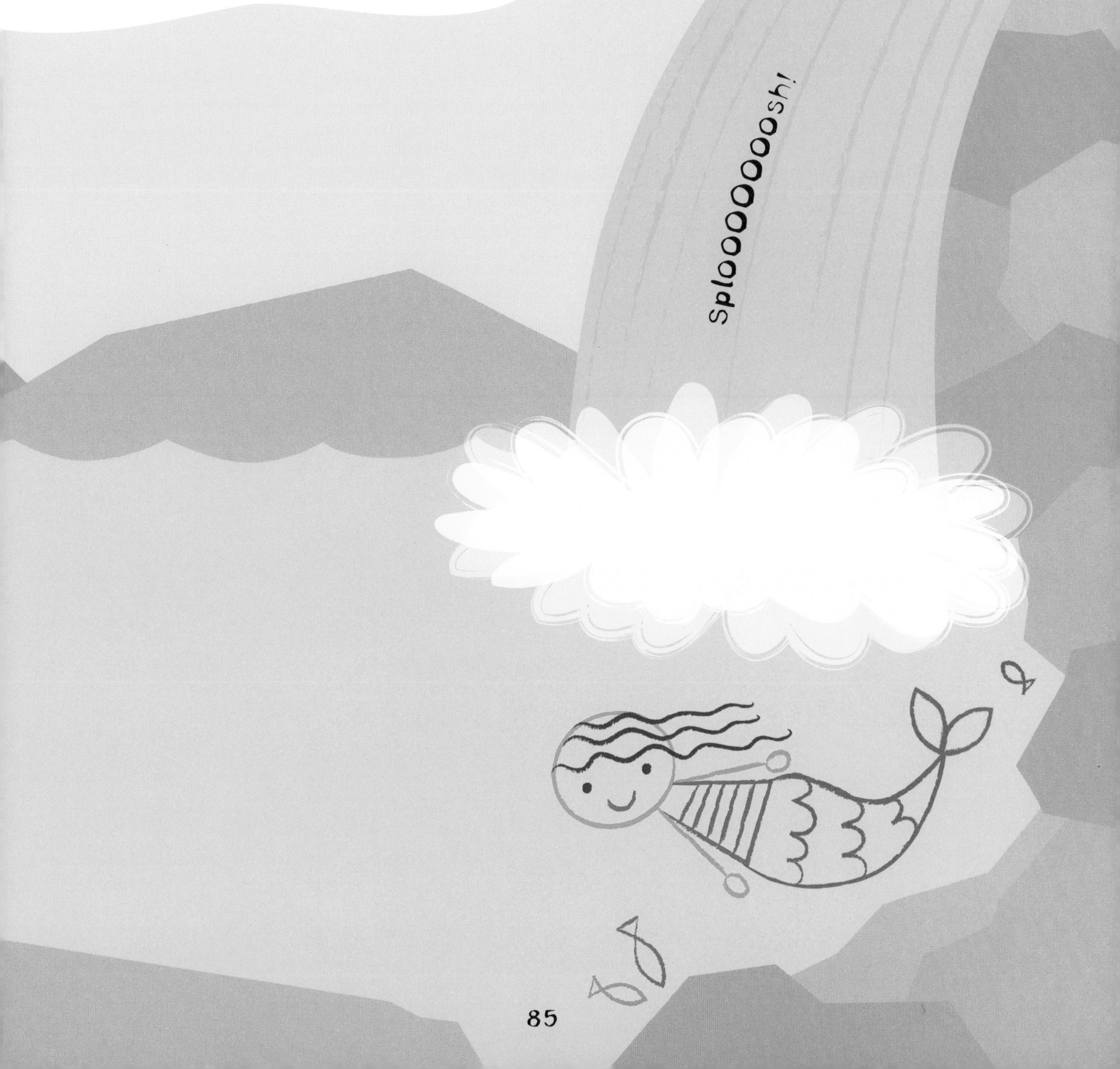
Splooooooosh!

Draw castles in the forest.

1

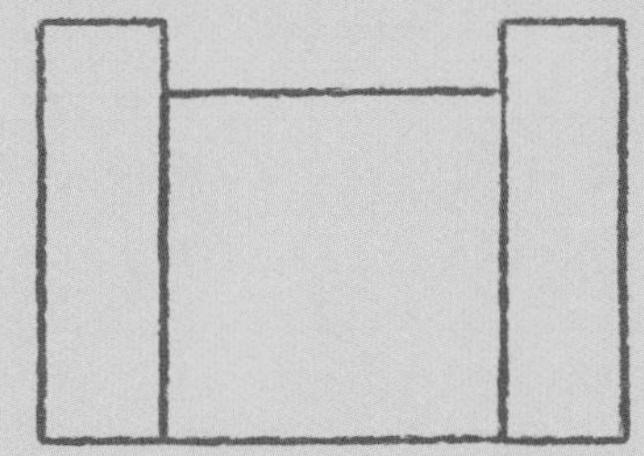

A square
and two rectangles....

2

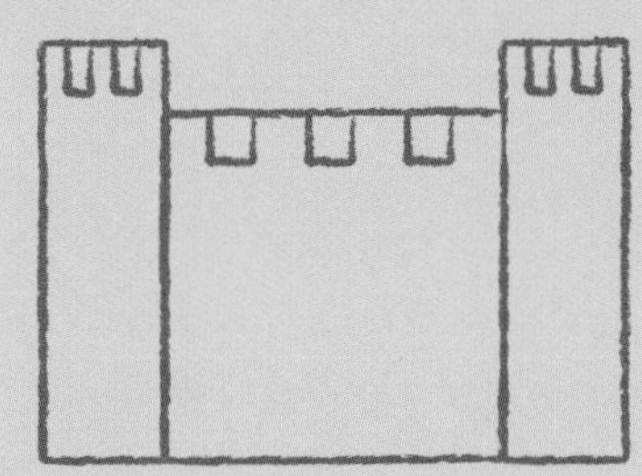

shapes along the walls...

3

triangles for roofs...

4

windows, a door and a flagpole...

5

narrow windows and a flag.

Finish the trees to look like this one.

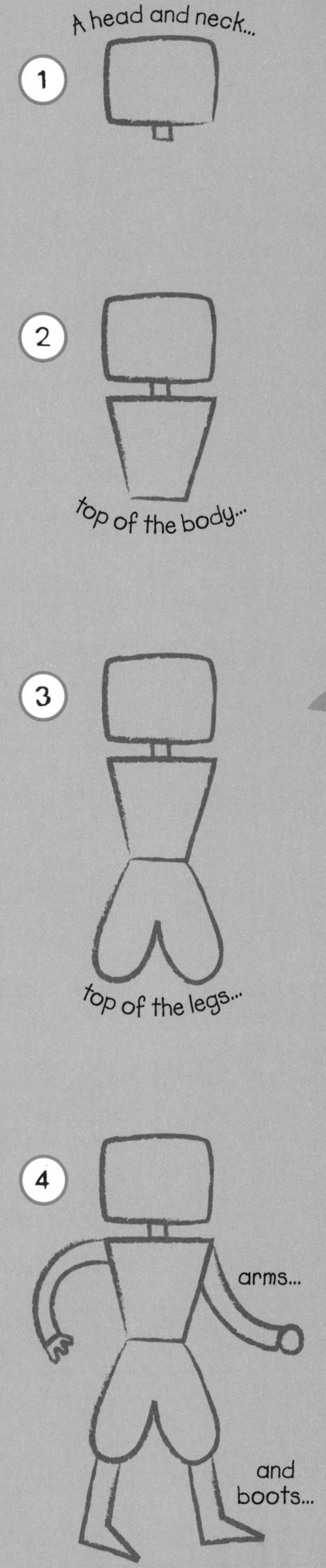

1
A head and neck...
2
top of the body...
3
top of the legs...
4
arms...
and boots...

Aaarrrrr!

Draw pirates on a tropical island.

a headscarf...

a face and eyepatch...

and a jacket and cutlass.

1
A head...
2
a long body and tail...
3
a wavy line...

Draw lizards crawling along branches.

Slurp!

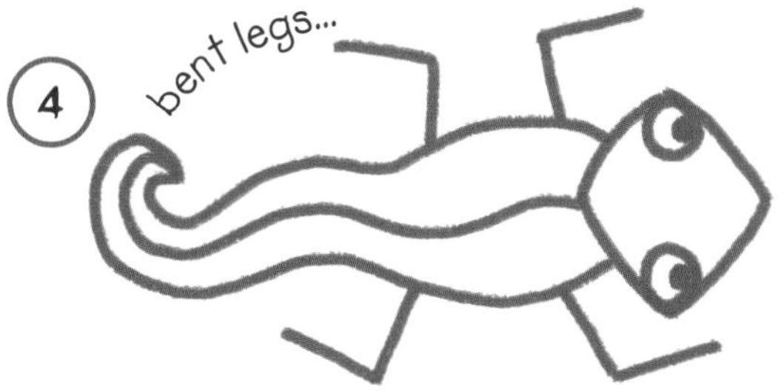
4
bent legs...

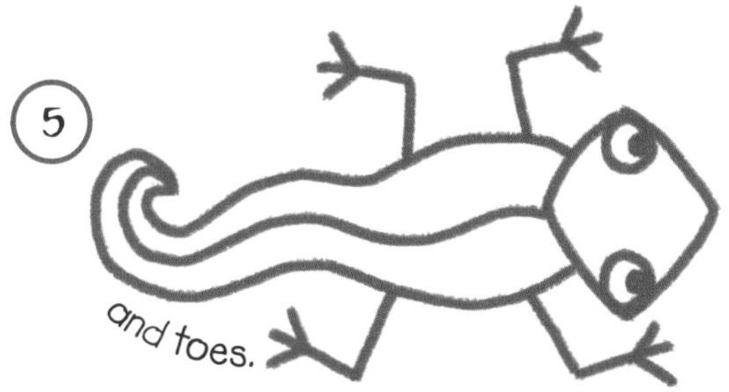
5
and toes.

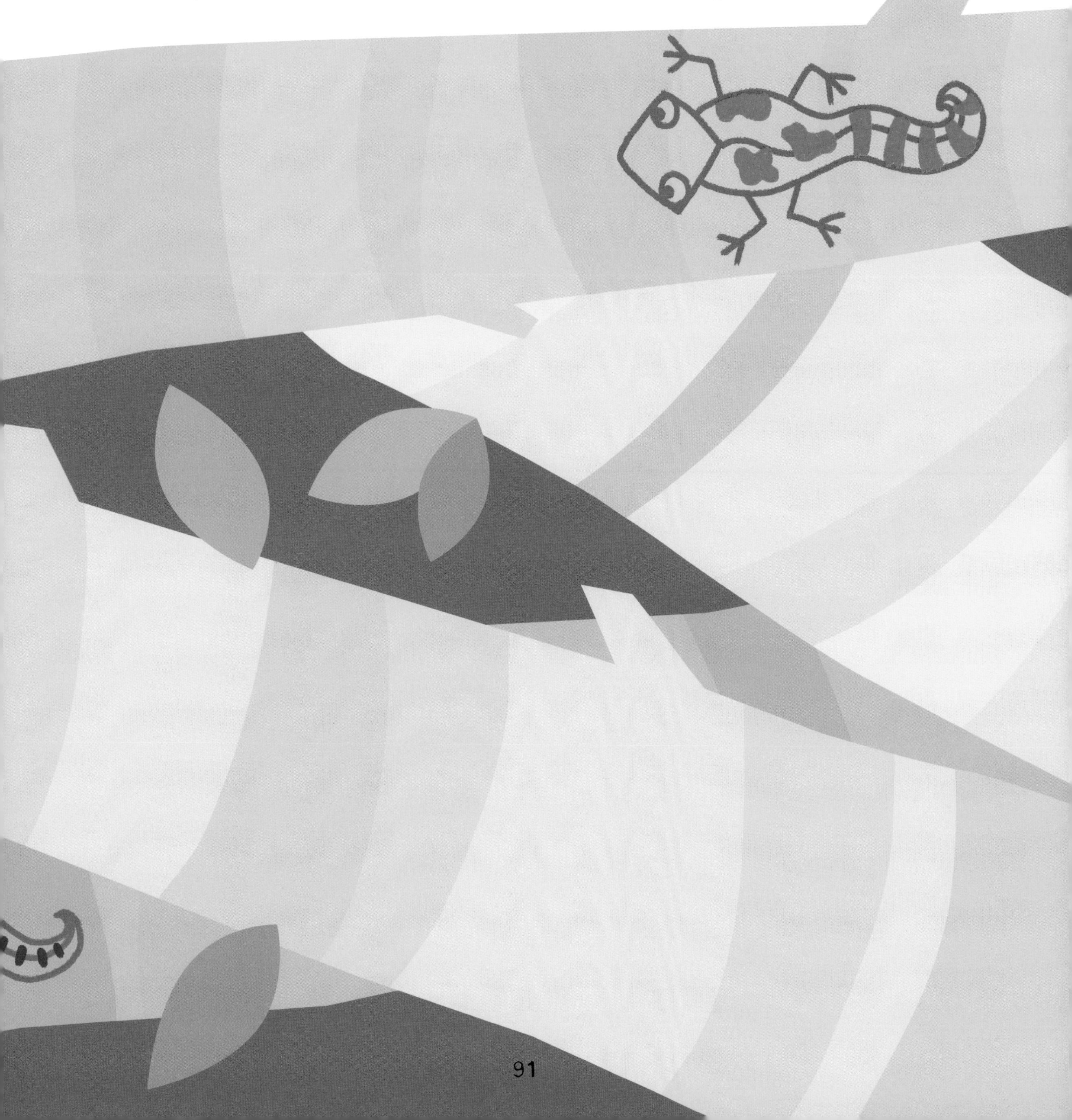

Draw reindeer in the snow.

1

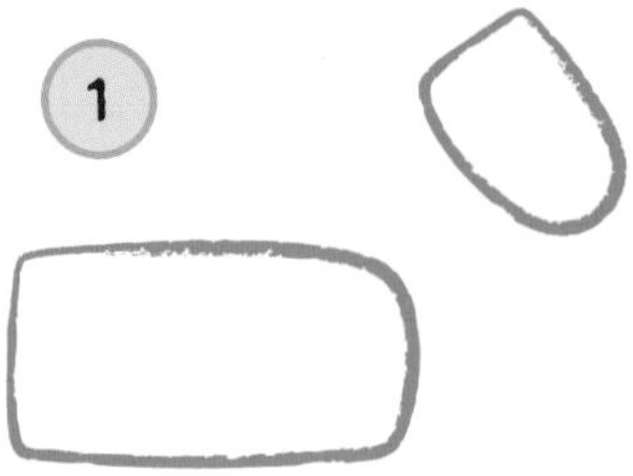

Draw a head and body....

2

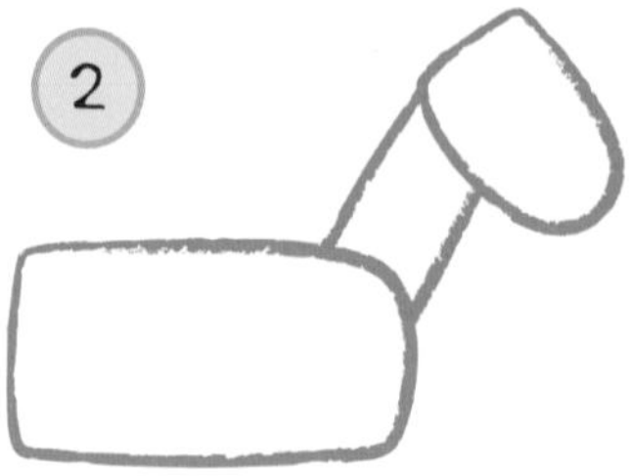

a neck...

3

and four legs.

Add patterns?

Closed eyes?

4
Draw a tail and ears...
5
antlers...
6
eyes and
a nose.

We need eyes and antlers.

Draw knights in a castle.

Halt!

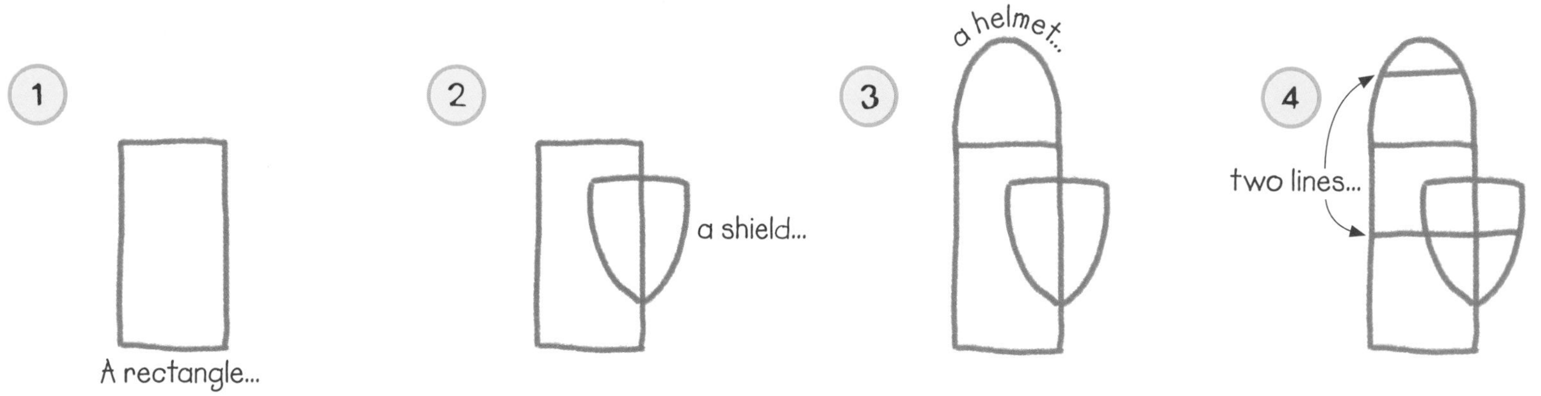
1
A rectangle...
2
a shield...
3
a helmet...
4
two lines...

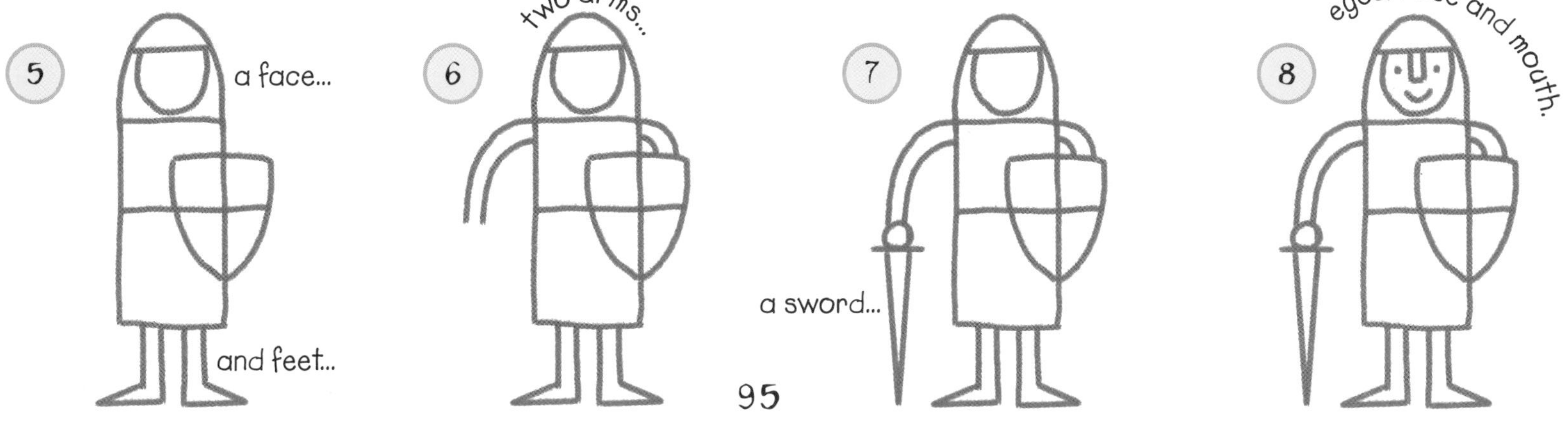
5
a face...
and feet...
6
two arms...
7
a sword...
8
eyes, nose and mouth.

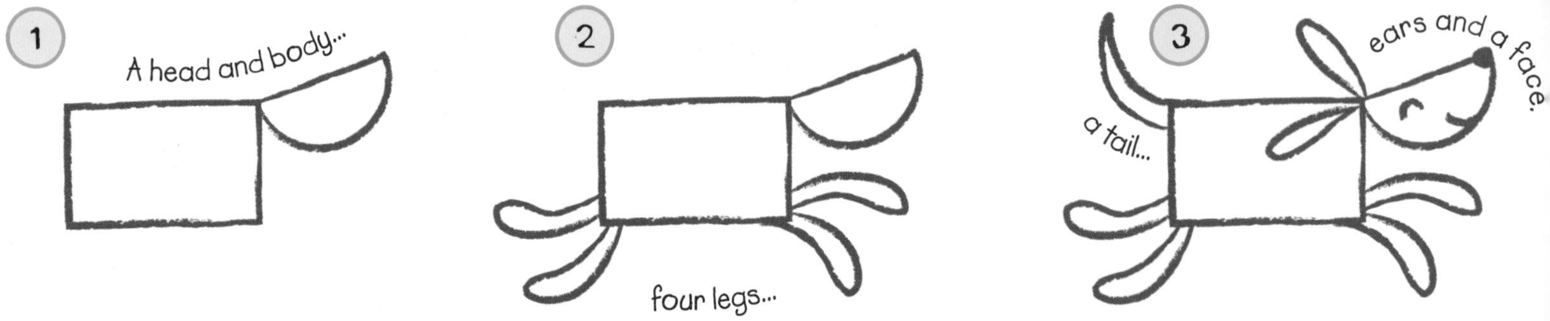
1
A head and body...
2
four legs...
3
a tail...
ears and a face.

Woof!
Squawk!
Meow!

Draw dogs chasing a ball, birds and a cat.

First published in 2012 by Usborne Publishing Ltd., 83-85 Saffron Hill, London, EC1N 8RT, England www.usborne.com

UE First published in America 2012.
Printed in China.